Behind the Lines

BEHIND THE LINES

STORIES BY J. T. WILSON

EXISLE
PUBLISHING

First published 2005

Exisle Publishing Limited,
P.O. Box 60-490, Titirangi, Auckland 1230.
www.exislepublishing.com

Copyright © J. T. Wilson 2005
J. T. Wilson asserts the moral right to be identified as the author of this work.

This is a work of fiction. The characters, incidents and dialogue are products of the author's imagination and are not to be construed as real. Any resemblance to actual events or persons, living or dead, is entirely coincidental.

All rights reserved. Except for short extracts for the purpose of review, no part of this book may be reproduced, stored in a retrieval system or transmitted in any form or by any means, whether electronic, mechanical, photocopying, recording or otherwise, without prior written permission from the publisher.

A catalogue record for this book is available from the National Library of Australia and from the National Library of New Zealand.

ISBN 0-908988-44-3

Text design and production by *BookNZ*
Cover design by Dexter Fry
Printed in China through Colorcraft Ltd., H. K.

CONTENTS

INTRODUCTION	7
BREAKDOWN	9
THE PRICE OF LIVING	44
WAY DOWN BELOW	46
YOU LIE	79
HIGH FLYER	83
SOFT ASYLUM	88
RANDOM	109
CAUGHT OUT	112
DIAMONDS DON'T SHINE IN THE DARK	117
SUCCESS	120
TAKING THE FALL	125
FLIGHT 109	136
AFTER MIDNIGHT	145

Introduction

FOR THREE YEARS NOW I have made my living selling my stories on the streets in many different places all over Australia and New Zealand, from Auckland to Adelaide, Melbourne to Wellington, Bondi Beach to Byron Bay, Brisbane to Newtown, and on university campuses everywhere.

It's been both fun and an extremely rewarding experience, but not without its hardships. Like landing in Sydney my first time out of New Zealand, with just $150 to my name and having to spend almost all of it on the bus ride into the city and on my first few nights' accommodation and food before finding a place to work in Newtown. Or having to wear my friend Rosie's clothes sometimes because I hadn't been selling enough stories to replace my own worn-out gear. And yes, sometimes even having to wonder where my next meal was coming from.

But these things happen to a lot of travellers and they are far outweighed by the good things – all the cool places I've seen and the many thousands of great people I've met while out selling my work. It's been a great chapter in my life, and I'm very thankful for every moment of it.

There have been so many strange and wonderful experiences, so many times when, even though things seemed impossible, something would always happen to save me from doubting my path. Whether it was a kind lady who gave me an apple one day in Glebe when I was feeling a little down and told me, 'You sitting there selling your stories gives other people hope that real people can make it in this world.' Or in Melaney, in southern Queensland, where we arrived stone cold broke and starving hungry and everything was closed except a local restaurant that had a $6.90 special on between five and seven, and we set up the stall at half past six on the deserted street and the one person who did come past bought three stories for $14.

People in the media have been a great help too: Justine at Triple J, Column 8 and Alexa Moses at the *Sydney Morning Herald*, Carolyn Webb at *The Age* in Melbourne, *The Glebe*, ABC television in Adelaide, the *Otago Daily Times* in Dunedin. Sometimes I would have starved had these people not written such kind things.

There are so many great creative people out there, and so many talented writers who don't seem able to find a place to be heard. Perhaps this is a way some of them may now choose. I hope so. It would be so positive in five years to see people out selling their work and building their own audiences. Then they would know that when people say you can't make money out of writing or any other creative activity, they don't have to believe it, that there are ways to be successful if they're willing to trust, and follow, their own path wholeheartedly.

So here they are, from the streets to you – my best stories all polished up and gathered together for the first time. I'm very proud of this collection. It brings together and showcases my work in a way that I was never able to do without the help of professional editors and any sort of real budget. It includes a few of the older stories, like 'The Price of Living' and 'Way Down Below', that I've sold so many copies of on the street, as well as many new ones including 'High Flyer', 'Soft Asylum', 'Breakdown', 'Taking the Fall', 'Flight 109', and the longest and newest of all, 'After Midnight'.

Thanks again to everyone who has bought my stories and helped to keep me living, learning and writing all this time.

J. T. Wilson

Breakdown

'WHAT'S THAT? What's that noise? Shit, not again.'

David could hear the noise too. It had started a few minutes before and had been getting slowly louder. He had been hoping it would go away. 'You put petrol in, didn't you? I told you we needed ...'

'Of course I did. You saw me put it in, didn't you, and the gauge is still way above half so it's not that.' David took a big breath; it could still go away ... but no. They were at the bottom of a big hill now and the van was losing more and more power and the first noise had been joined by lots of other smaller and more sinister ones. There was no way they were going to make it up the hill. David pulled over and turned the engine off.

'What are we going to do?' Nikki asked. 'We're miles away from anything!'

'I knew that bloody mechanic was dodgy,' David burst out. 'Two thousand bucks he charged us, for a gasket, and what else? A con rod! What the hell is that anyway? I'd like to go back and give him con rod.'

'It doesn't matter now,' Nikki said.

'Doesn't it?'

'No.' David looked at her. She was angry too but she was doing that *I am mad but I might not be and that is my superiority* face that just pissed him off even more. He wondered for a second if he should try and force her anger out, but what was the point? 'I don't know what we're going to do,' he admitted. 'Go for help I guess. There's nothing we can do ourselves.' He looked away from her out the window. Was she going to say it? That they should have brought Steve along with them. That he would have known what to do.

'What's the time?' he asked, sitting up a little. 'If we look at the map and make a few calculations we should be able to work out where we are at least.'

'Half past two.'

'Right, we left Ballina at a quarter to two and we have been averaging about ninety-five kilometres an hour.'

'Eighty-five – the speedo's out.'

'Okay eighty-five.' He picked up the map and unfolded it out over the steering wheel. 'That means that in three-quarters of an hour we would have covered about sixty kilometres, and the scale on this map is for fifty kilometres, so sixty per cent of one hundred is sixty and half of that is thirty which is about that much.' He measured the distance with his finger. 'So that means we must be about here. At the bottom of Flinders Hill, right before this town: Bangalow. Yes, here, look.' He pointed at the map. 'We passed that river just a few minutes ago and it's right before this corner so Bangalow must be right over the other side of this hill.'

David studied Nikki for a moment. 'You look tired. Why don't I walk over there and get some help? You can stay here. Have a lie down if you want.'

'Will you ring the mechanic?' she asked.

'That prick we went to in Ballina?'

'Yes.'

'Not a chance in hell. He's not getting another cent of our money.'

'But wasn't there a guarantee?'

'No.'

'But you said ...'

'I know what I said.' He folded the map, stepped out of the van and shut the door behind him. What more could he say? '*Sorry, he was the only guy in town that could do it on such short notice, that it was the only way out*'? He was sick of having to justify his actions to her like some naughty schoolboy just because she was the one with all the money. He started up the hill.

Sixty-four kilometres, three hundred and twenty-two metres back down the road, mechanic Nathan Ashcroft picked up the telephone and pushed number three on his speed dial. 'Alex?'

'Yes.'

'Another two headed your way – English, a couple. Usual deal – I left the bolts loose on the right cylinder head and a nut in the casing so they will lose power at the bottom of Flinders Hill. They shouldn't be far away now.'

'What year is the van?'

'Oh, you're going to love this. It's a genuine '59, with the split windscreen, the folding side doors and the small window at the back. It even has the mechanical indicators! They said they got it for six thousand from a great-aunt or something in Melbourne, but I reckon it would go for more than ten grand on the UK market. It's one of the best I've ever seen – Charlie will love it.'

'Good, if it all goes okay we'll have the six vans we need to fill the containers and I can ring Charlie in Sydney and my friend Robbo down in Victoria to arrange transportation. Well done, Nathan.'

Alex put the phone down and returned as calmly as he could to greasing the crankshaft on his workbench. Nathan was excited, but his part in this was over and, even if they did get caught, he had his three garages insured up to the hilt and no family, wife or parents to miss anyway, only his precious hunting in the weekends. But Alex did, so it was absolutely imperative that he did not act out of character when the English couple arrived. Any suspicion could ruin five long years of planning and risking everything, and take away the only chance he and Jenny had at a better life.

Alex could see the forecourt through a small window. The garage was busy today: in just a few minutes two cars pulled in for gas, a couple on a bike filled up and brought some food from the shop and then, finally, when it was all quiet again, he caught his first glance of David Williams staring curiously at the garage from across the road. Alex always knew when it was the person or people he was waiting for. It was something about the way they looked. He listened carefully as David talked with the petrol attendant, then to every step as they made their way through to the workshop.

'Hello ... excuse me.'

Alex paused, took a deep breath, put down the spanner and picked up a big old rag that could once have been red and turned around.

'Hey, what can we do for you?'

'Hi, me and my girlfriend, our van broke down over the hill.'

'What happened?'

'I'm not sure. We were just driving along when it started making these weird sounds.'

'What kind of sounds?' Alex had begun taking the grease off his fingers with the rag.

'Well, there was a kind of slopping sound I guess, then we just started losing power.'

'What kind of van is it?'

'A Volkswagen Kombi.'

'What year?'

''59.'

''59!' Alex whistled in a way that any small town mechanic might. 'They're getting rare these days.'

'Yeah, we got it cheap. A genuine one lady owner in Melbourne. A friend of my girlfriend's mother's sister. It's been a good runner too, for most of it.'

'And you want me to take a look at it then?'

'Yes.'

'Today?'

'Yes.'

'Shit, ah ... sorry, mate, but I can't help you there. I've got to finish getting this crankshaft greased then back into that tractor for Harvey Wilson down the road, that'll take me to half past eight as it is, and then I've got a list of things to get through tomorrow as long as your arm. It's harvest time, see, and everyone's making sure their equipment's up to scratch.'

'But we're stuck,' David insisted.

'It won't go at all?'

'No.'

'Oh, well that makes it tough.'

'What if we paid you extra?' David realised this was a bold offer given it wasn't his money he was making it with, yet he was sure Nikki would rather pay extra than sleep on the side of the road.

'Sorry mate, but it's not about money. It's a matter of time.'

'So there's nothing you can do?'

'Not right now, but if you're willing to wait, maybe I could take a look late tomorrow afternoon if I get a moment.'

'Okay, but what about now, what can we do now?'

Alex paused and took a deep breath. He had given an outstanding performance so far, but it wasn't something that came naturally, even if the character he was playing was himself. 'There's Henry, the petrol attendant. He could come down the hill and tow you back when he's finished at about seven.'

'And you're sure you wouldn't reconsider if we gave you some extra cash?' David asked.

Nathan Ashcroft had pushed Alex on this point before, encouraging him to take the travellers for everything he could, but Alex had insisted that the line had to be drawn somewhere. He had to sleep at night, after all.

'Sorry mate, but that's the best I can do. In the meantime you could hole up over the road. The pub puts on a pretty good feed, and the rooms aren't too nasty.'

'And will the van be safe here overnight?' David asked.

'No problems so far, but if you're worried about it we can leave it inside the garage.'

'Any idea how much it will cost?'

'Sorry mate, but there's no way of knowing until I've looked at it. Speculating has got me into too much trouble over the years so I don't take the risk any more.' This time Alex was only half lying, and he could feel the truth warm his insides a little. As he told his wife Jenny, if he had been a luckier man with more ability or capital at his disposal he might have always been able to tell the truth. But a small town garage just didn't get enough honest business.

When David arrived back at the van an hour later he found Nikki asleep in the back. He wanted to wake her right away but instead opened the side door and sat quietly on the step. Her feet were just inches from his head and he could hear the breath enter and leave her body in the intimacy of the small space. In her mind, if she had money she was safe, things were okay. She didn't see all the other things that had to be done after the money had been paid. All that was someone else's job. This was sometimes a little hard for David to deal with, partly because of all the extra work he had to do in their everyday life, but mostly because all her friends and family were the same: all they saw when they looked as him was a fumbling wannabe artist boyfriend who borrowed Nikki's hard-earned money and never paid it back, which was bullshit because he always did.

And who the hell were they to presume to know how everything worked, anyway? How did they know how artists, successful or starving, fitted into the grand scheme of things. For all they knew, artists could be the very glue that kept their stinking consumerist lifestyle together. And yet, 'You have to work like my parents and their parents and their parents before them,' she might say when she woke up or, worse, 'You've tried long enough with your art, David. Everyone else has a car and a house already. You're so far behind. It's time to make some real money, time to live in the real world.' And he owed her so much now maybe she did have the right to tell him that. 'Ah, fuck!' He moved away from the van in frustration, but as he did his feet made a noise on the gravel and she began to stir. No, he thought, don't wake up. He couldn't talk to her now. He moved around behind the van where she couldn't see him.

He hated money. Even the people in his world, where the sale of a painting for a thousand pounds could keep you alive and happy and working for a month or two, had to bow to money. Or did they? Maybe he could write a note, do a runner. Let her parents enjoy the fruition of the conviction they had never been moved to hide. Let them tell their daughter she was wrong, that he really was just a scumbag all along. Why not? What did she really care?

David imagined the note: it would only have to say that someone was coming down later and that she could have his half of the van. There it is, damn you, he thought, smiling. It's all friggin' yours. That would teach her for doing what she did to Steve in the shower ...

'David?' He didn't move. 'David, is that you?' He shook his head. She was awake and if she saw him now she would be frightened. She might have already picked up on his energy. 'David!' Yes, she was scared. He could hear it in her voice. He didn't want her to be scared. He wanted to protect her, to comfort her and make everything okay. Steve Wilcox wasn't here to do that. He walked around the van. She looked soft now, her frightened face very different from the one he had been imagining just moments before.

'What's wrong, David?'

'The man at the garage, he said ...'

'You're angry, aren't you?'

'Ah ...'

'Yes. You went and got yourself all worked up again, didn't you?' she said with a smile. She liked talking to him like this.

'I ... I ...' He wanted to deny it, to get out of her tractor beam, but it was too late. She was pulling him in.

'Come here, Davy, come on.' He resisted again, even began backing away, but she had already sat up and her hands were on him. 'You can make love to me if you want,' she offered, putting his hand on her breast. 'That will make you feel better.'

'I ...' He was losing power to resist.

'Look,' she entreated. She was pulling down her jeans. She took his hand, put it inside her knickers. It was all over.

David didn't think another rebellious thought until they went to bed that night in the hotel room. Life was safe with Nikki and not without its satisfactions, but maybe there were other things he was meant to be doing, other paths he was meant to be following. It had been a long time since he had stepped out into the great unknown, let go and allowed the world to steer him. Too long perhaps. A shiver. Life before her had been no picnic either. Some of the days had been dark and cold and lonely and maybe they would be like that again. Should he take the risk? Would it be worth it when it was so hard to leave, and so final, and when he looked out into the world without her all he could see was darkness.

The next morning David woke early and left the room without waking Nikki. She always slept longer than him and he enjoyed the time by himself. There wasn't much to the town – six or seven shops maybe. One that sold gumboots and farming work gear on one side, with the latest 'city fashion' on the other. Another selling fish and chips, pizza and chicken. There was also a general store/video shop, an appliance store, a bakery and of course the garage. David stopped a moment there. The garage had seemed shut when he first glanced at it, but when he looked at it a second time he realised that there was a light on: he could see the naked bulb hanging from the tin roof inside the workshop. The mechanic must have started early to get through everything so he would have time to work on Nikki's van. Maybe he would get it done earlier than he had estimated. This made David feel a little excited and he was about to turn away and carry on when something else caught his eye. The car in front of the garage. A red station wagon, unremarkable except for a brightly coloured bumper sticker. He'd seen the car before somewhere, but where ...? He stared at it for a moment, but nothing came to mind so he dismissed it and turned away.

David became conscious for the first time that the main street was actually quite steep. The town itself was stuffed into the top of a small valley with the road disappearing over the top of the hill in one direction and flattening out onto the valley floor in the other. The main street must have been a river bed once, and all the little side streets small creeks where the tar now ran up, with two or three houses on each side. Even if all the houses were full of people there would still only be a few hundred in the town. As it left the town, the road was bordered by tall trees on either side, then sprawled out over the countryside, crossing paddocks and little bridges before fading into the distance.

The bakery was open now so David bought two croissants, then an avocado and a lemon from the fruit shop to squeeze over it. The anger he felt toward Nikki was gone now and it would be nice to share something delicious for breakfast. He was about to walk back into the hotel when he swung round. The red station wagon was gone.

Nikki wanted to go over to the garage earlier but David insisted they wait until at least five o'clock.

'Why?' she asked.

'Because he said he was busy, and there's no point going over and interrupting his rhythm. We're only going to slow him down and besides, I don't want to seem pushy.'

'Pushy?' she said. 'Who's being pushy? The sooner we know what's going on the better. If we leave it too long it will be too late to leave and we'll be stuck here another night.'

At five o'clock David walked over the road to the garage and found Alex at the workbench again, working on what looked like the same piece of metal. When Alex turned around he seemed a little bit embarrassed.

'Ah, sorry mate, but I haven't had a chance to look at it yet.'

'But you said ...' David began.

'Yes, I know, but I have just been so flat out I haven't had a chance.'

'So when do you think you might ...?'

'Well, to be honest, if you'd asked me an hour ago I would have said I'd get round to it tonight, but Teddy Watson just rang me and said his harvester has done a coil and he needs it up and running by tomorrow afternoon so I'm probably going to be out there until late tonight.'

'And tomorrow?'

'Well, let's see, there's the Ferguson job, and Johnny Martin's Bedford should take me most of the day. Why don't you come in about this time again? I can't promise you anything, but we might have been able to at least have a look at it by then.' David looked at him a moment. He really wanted to push, and he could hear Nikki in the back of his mind telling him he should, but he could also see that it made no sense to do so.

Back in the hotel room, Nikki was sitting on the bed and looked eager to hit the road.

David sighed. This was not going to be easy. 'Not until tomorrow.'

'Tomorrow? But he said ...'

'Yes, I know.'

'Well, can't he hurry it up? What's he doing? What if we offer him some extra money?'

'I already did, yesterday.'

She flashed her eyes at him. 'And it didn't make him want to do it sooner?' She was surprised.

'No, it's not about money. He's got other jobs to do.'

'Well, is there anybody else?'

David looked at the map. 'Not until Byron Bay and it would cost a fortune to get towed there. No, I think we're stuck here.'

But the next day, when David went back to talk to Alex, he got the same answer as he had the day before. The same thing happened the next day, and the next. This was tolerable at first. He and Nikki had chores to do, like washing, and then washing all the little things they usually wore when doing their washing. But then, as the little things began to run out, so did their patience.

'Okay, okay,' Alex conceded on the fifth day when David had become angry himself. 'I've been mucking you guys around a bit. I'll look at it tonight, I promise. I won't go home until I can tell you exactly what's wrong with it.'

'No wonder you didn't get up the hill,' he told David and Nikki next morning as they followed him to the engine bay at the back of the van. 'I'm surprised it even ran at all. There's a gap between the head and block on one of the cylinder heads big enough to stick a slice of toast in.' David and Nikki stared at him blankly. 'Look,' he continued, pointing at the engine, 'Volkswagen make their engines so that the pistons go off to the side instead of up and down. The engine design is called a flat four, see – two cylinders on this side and two on the other. Well, the steel case, which is called the block, see here, is made out of two main parts and if these two parts aren't held together really tightly then the engine won't run.'

'How much does it cost to fix?' Nikki asked coldly, after a silence.

'It's not worth fixing,' Alex answered. 'Even if you did seal it back together there's another noise. I could hear it when I tried to turn it over, something bad. I think you've snapped the crankshaft or something, maybe even a couple of con rods. It happens quite a lot. When something major breaks in an engine like this it leaves too much work for the other things to do and they buckle under the weight of the extra pressure.'

There was another silence.

'You're serious? It's really not worth fixing?' Nikki asked.

'No.'

'And what about another motor?'

'Too expensive.'

'How much?'

'Another couple come in about a year and a half ago with a similar thing and I priced a new motor for them and it was just under twelve thousand dollars, including import duties. You have to order them direct from Germany you see, there's no other way.'

'Twelve thousand! And there are no second-hand ones?'

'Not a chance. You just can't get them anymore, not for Kombis this old.'

'So what are we going to do?' Nikki asked.

'Get the bus,' offered Alex. 'Save yourself the hassle.'

'But what about the van? We can't just leave it. Shit!' Her temper flared. 'We just spent two fucken grand on it and now it's worthless. Worse. We probably can't even leave it on the side of the road – they'll check the registration and fine us.'

There was another even longer silence. David, feeling somehow more neutral that the van had been written off, started to watch Alex more closely. He was still handling that same oily red rag, and he seemed to be clutching it rather tightly.

'I could take it,' Alex offered. 'I don't usually buy vans, but maybe I could help you out. We've got some extra room out the back.'

David couldn't help but be a little suspicious. 'But if it's broken then what good is it to you?'

'Well, like I said, from time to time people like you come in and maybe some day someone will have a motor.'

'But you said there wasn't a chance in hell ...'

'There probably isn't. I was just trying to help ...' Alex looked at Nikki for support.

'Yes David. What's wrong with you? He's trying to help us.'

David shook his head. 'Sorry,' he said. 'I'm just disappointed, that's all.'

'Yes,' Alex agreed. 'It is disappointing.'

'So how much can you give us for it?' Nikki asked.

'Five hundred would be as high as I could go, plus I could waive the towing fee.'

Nikki and David looked at each other for a moment, then Nikki said, 'Right, we'll come back in an hour. I never buy or sell anything without going for a walk to think about it first.'

David tried to catch up with Nikki as she raced ahead of him across the road and then up the stairs and slammed the door behind her, leaving him standing on the landing. He could feel her anger, and 'Fuck this' and 'Fuck that' slipped out from under the door.

David looked back down the stairs. How cool would it be to take off now? Too cool, obviously, cold even, and he wouldn't dare, but just imagine. Leaving with nothing but what he had on. They were always surrounded by expensive bullshit she insisted they needed: vans and DVD players and stupid wooden furnishings. How great would it be to just let go of it all now and walk away?

Then the door handle turned and the lock was released. When he walked in Nikki was sitting on the bed, looking serious. It wasn't over yet.

'So what are we going to do?' she asked. 'I've got five months left in Australia, five months that I was going to spend driving around in that van. I loved that van. It was an original '59, a peace wagon. It even had the split windscreen, the small lights at the back – everything. But twelve thousand bucks, I can't afford that, and even if I could I'd be stupid to pay it.' She paused. 'That rude bastard. How long did he take to tell us that? It would have only taken him two minutes to figure it out. But no, five days he makes us wait. Five bloody days in this shit hole, and then he's got the cheek to offer us five hundred bucks. We should have sold it as soon as we got problems. We were stupid to spend two thousand bucks on it. Thailand is definitely out of the question now. I'll have to go straight home to the UK unless I borrow money from my parents.'

Thailand was another sore point between them. David had never had the money to go. He was going to stay in Sydney and work for a couple of months, save up some money and then meet her at home. But saving to get home now would be the least of his problems. He had pitched in two thousand dollars for her 'dream van', money he didn't have, money that she had lent him thinking that they would get it back and more when they sold the Kombi. 'All you're buying is the risk,' she told him when they set out.

But that risk had cost him a thousand-dollar debt to her in Ballina for those repairs and now another two thousand dollars because even though he hadn't bought the van, he had agreed that, as his contribution, he would be equally liable. Now he owed her more than four thousand dollars: he had clocked up just over another thousand for this and that along the way to. Money he had planned to pay back on the sale of the van. Money he didn't now have the means to get. And how long, he wondered now, was it going to be before she started on that?

'Five hundred bucks!' she continued. 'Do you know how much those Kombis are worth in the UK? I'd get ten grand for it, and that's pounds, David, pounds!'

Nikki kept on and on until finally she began to slow down, then stopped and looked at David in silence. The anger had gone from her eyes now but they still seemed to want something from him. He excused himself from the room and walked downstairs to the mini kiosk in the back corner of the restaurant where you could help yourself to free tea and coffee. By the time he returned and handed her the cup of tea her eyes were less demanding and he could feel that she had made a decision.

'If things were different,' she conceded. 'If we were in England, Scotland or even France someone might have been able to come and help us and we wouldn't have to sell that beautiful, beautiful van, but we're not and I guess we just have to accept that.'

'You're going to sell it?'

'We have to.'

An hour later they had picked up the money, packed up their things and were walking towards the outskirts of the small town to stick out their thumb. David had rung the bus company but they didn't come through until late that night and they didn't want to wait. The third car stopped and picked them up.

'Hop in,' said a red-faced farmer in a late model Falcon ute. 'My name's Richard. Where you guys heading?'

'Ah, hi, I'm Nikki and this is Dave. We're going to Byron Bay.'

'No worries. I am going to Suffolk Park which is right before Byron, but I can drop you guys off in town if you'd like. I'm not very busy today.'

'Cool, thanks,' said Nikki. 'That would be great.'

Richard helped them lift their bags up onto the back of the ute, then pulled back out onto the road.

'Where you guys from?' he asked.

'Kent.'

'Oh nice. I went there once, had a great-aunt who lived in Pennington Road.'

'And what about you?' Nikki asked. 'Do you live at Suffolk Park?'

'I do now. I have a farm out near the Shannon and I used to live in the farmhouse there, but I got married a couple of years back and Hayley wasn't too fond of living in the country.'

'You're married?' Nikki was obviously impressed.

'Yeah, we thought we'd better make it official.'

'Wow, how exciting. Where did you guys meet?'

'We met in the Shannon. She was woofing for a mate down the road, you know, working for accommodation and food, that sort of thing, and when my mate ran out of work and she wanted to stay I said I had something for her. I didn't of course, I had to make up something for her to do, but I just fancied her so much I couldn't bear to see her go so soon.'

'Wow, cool.'

'Yeah, and what about you two?' David looked at Nikki: would she be bothered to tell the story of their coming together? Yes. Her mood must have changed because she sat up and talked enthusiastically about how her mother had wanted to have her hallway painted, and how she had this crazy idea that instead of hiring a painter she was going to support the local arts community by employing an artist to do it. 'They will do a better job of it anyway,' she had joked. 'And be cheaper.' And of course

David did do an excellent job in her house, but in more ways than she bargained for because the night after he had finished and picked up his pay he arrived on her doorstep again to pick up her daughter for their first 'official' date.

David zoned out about halfway through the retelling and began to stare out the window. There was a lot to think about. Fortunately Nikki had split the five hundred dollars from the van so he had that two hundred and fifty dollars plus another twenty-five of his own, but that was all the money he had, and a week's accommodation in Byron Bay would use up half of that. He would have to get a job, and he wasn't sure how Nikki would take that. She sure hadn't made any plans to stay there. Maybe she would tell him that he needed to borrow more money, but how could he do that?

He had paid for this trip with the money from a lucky piece of installation, an unusual piece he didn't really like, and he was just about to throw it out when a friend rang and said they needed something to fill a gap in their exhibition. He had only put a big price on it because it seemed such a long shot that anyone would actually buy it. But someone did buy it, and he spent that lucky money on his ticket to Australia, and it seemed wrong that now he should get so far into debt that he would not even be able to go back to what he was doing before he left. Still, maybe Nikki would like Byron Bay and be happy to stay there a while, or better yet maybe she would suggest that they split up for a while, that she go up north while he stayed there and worked. That would be really good. It was hard to be around someone he owed so much money, especially when they didn't really understand what it meant.

Richard dropped them off in the middle of town. David never liked booking ahead. There was only one thing worse than getting stuck in a small, dark, dingy, lifeless hostel and that was having to pay for it. Besides, David liked walking around town looking in different hostels. It was a nice way to get to a few places and onto a few streets he might not otherwise see. He left Nikki on the grass beside the beach with the bags. The excitement she had shown in the car when she was talking with Richard quickly dissipated when he left and suddenly she seemed tired and defeated again.

David walked into what seemed to be the middle of town. He had heard a lot about Byron Bay. There was apparently a large alternative community and a thriving local arts scene, but if there was he sure couldn't see it yet. There was some art for sale in a few shop windows, but it was that plastic kind, cheaply duplicated and produced by the ton for mass consumption. There was a cool photo in the window of a shop on the corner, though. It was blown up to poster size and mounted in a white frame with a caption below it that read 'Reef draining, Hawaii.' And it looked as if someone had just pulled the plug on the ocean and all the water was rushing out because there was a completely vertical wall of water standing like a huge step in the ocean. Five or six surfers had paddled out of its way and were lying on their boards a couple of hundred metres off watching. David looked at it for a long time. How random and fantastic.

The first hostel he came to claimed in big letters to be right beside the beach, and indeed he had left Nikki only a block back, but the big square concrete building seemed many miles away from anything like nature and the sea. The receptionist was friendly enough. 'Yeah, sure, no worries,' she answered when he asked if he could have a look around. The kitchen was nice, well equipped, but the lounge was a bit small and dark with shut curtains and a dozen sleepy video eyes that glared at him as if he had just robbed half their life force when he opened the door, and since the outdoor area on the roof was full of other young English twenty-somethings all happily toasting their good fortunes, there wouldn't be many other places to hang out.

A few hundred metres further up a side road he come across another larger hostel, but this time he regretted even asking to have a look around. As he walked away a girl whizzed past and offered him a small square piece of paper with 'free internet' written on it. What the hell. He could do with a break.

'Where are you going after Byron?' they asked him in the travel/internet shop. 'North or south? Why don't you have a look at this while you wait for the next available computer? It shouldn't be more than a few minutes.'

'Thank you.' He took the brochure and stared at the scenic island he hadn't a hope in hell of seeing in this lifetime.

At home David's close friends Kathy and Peter were going to have a baby. His granddad had been in hospital with another stroke. 'But don't worry,' his mother wrote. 'It was a very mild one. He was in and out within a few hours.' The weather was shit, raining every day, three or four people told him. He scrolled down. Good news! Sarah, a fellow artist, his ex-girlfriend, best friend and biggest fan, said that another one of his paintings had sold and that she would give him the money as soon as she could. She would have already, only none of her own work sold during the exhibition in a café where she had had to pay almost two hundred pounds to have them displayed, and as she was broke and needed to pay that before she got the paintings back, she had had to use the money from his painting. 'I've got a real job though for a couple of weeks now. So I'll have you paid back soon.' And she would too, because she would be working for her dad in east London and he always made sure that she was well compensated for her time. It was his way of giving her the help she was too stubborn to take. A thousand pounds he paid her some weeks, for looking over a few accounts and taking a couple of phone calls. David had never really been sure if she knew it was so much or not. If she did she didn't admit it. He thought he had seen her smile ironically once when she was talking about it, but he couldn't be sure. Anyway, this was great news. Two hundred pounds, less a bit for her efforts. He might get up to five hundred

Australian dollars. He could make that last a while – if he could last until the money arrived.

Out on the street again he stopped and looked around. He hadn't walked more than a few blocks from the roundabout and the beach where Nikki was waiting, but this part of Byron Bay was quite different. At the other end most of the people had been tourists, but here they were more spread out and there were locals as well. These people moved slower, less desperately, less ambitiously, in a way he was not used to. Byron Bay had a mind and life of its own. There was something more here to discover than just a few touristy pieces of art and a beach.

Groups of people were sitting in the park over the road, so David crossed the road to get a closer look. He was particularly taken with one circle of people in the middle, the relaxed and extremely casual way two or three of them came and went without any apparent explanation. It all seemed so very comfortable, so happy.

Then he stopped. He hadn't seen her until right then, but now he had no idea how on earth he could possibly have missed her. She was sitting on the other side of the group. She looked a little bit like the others, with similar clothes and had similar hair, but she was completely different, from them, from him, from everything. He couldn't take his eyes off her or understand how the others could be so near her and not be staring as well. He walked up to the edge of the group. The girl was smiling at him and he was smiling back and he could feel the people exchanging glances. It felt amazing. It was as if he had just climbed out of a long stuffy train ride into a cool breeze or finally found the light in a dark place, and they could all see it too. They couldn't miss it. It was as though he and the girl were two stones banged together and the air between them was full of the sparks. He wanted to walk right over and kiss her, and had a feeling they might all clap if he did.

He couldn't just stand there. He thought for a moment. 'Oh, hey,' he said. 'Do you guys know a good place to stay?' They all looked at each other and then turned around and said all at once, 'The Arts Factory', then laughed. David laughed too. The Arts Factory. It sounded good already. He turned and stared walking away, but stopped and turned back again. They were all still looking at him. He lifted his hand and started pointing, hoping they would play along. Yes, 'warm' they said, then no, they were shaking their heads, 'cold'. He went left again ... yes, they nodded, further, yes, bingo. The Arts Factory was that way. He turned and carried on walking, but stopped when he was sure that they had gone back to what they were doing before he arrived. And yes, she was still looking at him.

Beside the bus stop there was a map and he stopped to look it up. The Arts Factory? Yes, there it was. He sketched down a rough copy of the map on a piece of paper from his wallet and set out. There wasn't much to it: a railway line which he could see already, then two lefts and a right. He walked over the tracks and took the first left. The Byron Bay he had seen so far ended quickly. Here the houses were small and quaint, more like a holiday village than a big town.

After the first block the houses thinned out even more and he started to get an idea of just how small the town was. He turned left, right and then at the end of the road saw a sign saying 'The Piggery'. He walked through the car park and up to the Arts Factory reception.

'Hey, you guys got any vacancies?'

'Sure, how long do ya want to stay?' said a friendly voice, and without having to look around or think about it or anything David knew that he would stay there for a while. He made the reservation then headed back to the beach. He had kept Nikki waiting long enough.

As he walked, two things filled David's mind. The first was Nikki. He had been away for a while and she had not been in a good mood when he left. Would she bite his head off when he got back? He was getting sick of that, he used to like the fact that she was a bit controlling – it was fun, a game – but now he was over it, really over it. The other thing in his mind was that girl in the park. She was really something. He hadn't even needed to speak to her to know that. He hoped to see her again soon, and he had a feeling he would.

He turned the corner at the top of town and suddenly stopped. He could see Nikki sitting on the grass, but she was not alone. She was surrounded by people and he had seen them before. Yes ... yes ... oh my God, it was the group from the park, and she was there too. What should he do? Would Nikki know? Would she sense that something was up between them? He turned and looked down the street, maybe he should bail, come back later when they had gone? Yes. No. Shit. It was too late. Nikki had seen him. He walked up, sat in their circle and listened quietly to their conversation, both trying not to look at that girl, and stealing every glance he could without Nikki seeing.

She told him on the way to the Arts Factory that she liked it here so far, that even though these weren't really her type of people she liked how everyone was so friendly, and that if it was all right with him, she wouldn't mind staying in Byron for a while.

'Cool,' he said. 'I might even get some work while we're here. Or better yet·do some painting.'

'Great,' she said flatly. Her thoughts had moved on. But yes, things were finally starting to work out.

After they had pitched the tent Nikki disappeared into the shower, leaving David to have a look around. The Arts Factory was massive – '16 acres' the sign out the front said. There was a main building with a pool in the middle and dorm rooms all around it, a sand-pit, two teepees, a lake and an island camping area where huts were made out of two lengths of pipe folded over at the top into a half circle, then covered with two layers of thick painted canvas. The floors were all part of a single boardwalk that went right around the lake. There was a women's space too, a cafeteria, a canteen, the reception area, a bar, a pool room and, of course, The Piggery. Once a slaughterhouse for pigs, the big old building was now a character restaurant and cinema, with a bar and beer garden at one end, and a couple of natural remedy shops at the other. In the carpark between the piggery and the Arts Factory there were a line of pay phones, a bike stand where you could hire bikes and a notice board. David stopped there to look. Yes, here was something useful. A ride to the Shannon markets on Saturday the 28th. That was tomorrow. He found a pen in his pocket – he always had at least one or three there to chew on since he gave up smoking two years ago. He could ring right now. If he got to the markets he could have a look at the art and get an idea of whether his work would sell there. He walked over to the phone, put a couple of bucks in and dialled the number.

'Hello.'

'Yeah, hi, I'm ringing about the ad on the notice board at the Arts Factory.'

'Hang on, sorry I can't hear you, my cellphone is a bit funny, oh wait ... yeah, there, now I can hear you. Who is this?'

'It's David speaking. I am ringing about the ad ...'

'Oh, hey, David. You want to come to the Shannon markets tomorrow?'

'Yes. Me and my girlfriend.'

The voice on the other end of the phone seemed puzzled for a moment. 'David, is your girlfriend's name Nikki?'

'Yes, but how did you ...'

'Hey David, this is Jess. We met you guys down at the beach this afternoon, well we met you in the park actually. You were pretty quiet at the beach.'

David just about dropped the phone. It was her. It was the girl from the park. 'Wow ... ah ... Jess,' he said.

'Yeah, looks like were meant to see a bit more of each other.'

There was a silence. David didn't know what to say to this. Maybe this was a gift, a chance to get to know her without the intensity. Why not? He had to take things as they come, right? 'Yes,' he answered. 'Cool coincidence.'

'Coincidence?' she asked. 'You don't believe in fate?'

'I ... ah ...? I'm not sure. I believe in something and ...' David paused; there wasn't much more time left on the phone 'Maybe I can tell you about it tomorrow. Jess, I've got a question I'd like to ask you.'

'Shoot.'

'These markets ... see I'm an artist. Do you think that if I did a few paintings ... well ... do you think I could take them along and sell them? Do you think people there would buy them?

'Tomorrow?' she asked.

David laughed. 'No, no, not tomorrow. Maybe in a week or two.'

'Well yeah, sure, why not? Everybody else does.'

'So what time are you guys heading up there?' he asked.

'You want to come?'

'Yes. Is that all right?'

'Yeah sure, no problem. Tomorrow we want to get up there early. Jo has made some fire pois to sell.'

'Fire pois?'

'Yeah, they're a New Zealand thing. They're a chain with a handle at one end and a ball of fire at the other and you swing them around. You've never seen them before?'

'No.'

'Well then, tonight's the night. We're doing a fire dancing display in the park. Why don't you come down and watch?'

Nikki and David spent the next couple of hours getting food from the supermarket and cooking dinner. David couldn't help feeling a little guilty for not telling her what he was up to, and was relieved when she said she was tired and might have an early night. 'Good idea,' he agreed. 'You've had a big day. I might go for a walk. Someone told me there are heaps of buskers out at night and I could do with seeing some live music.' Nikki went to bed about half an hour later and David stayed long enough to make sure she was comfortable, then kissed her good night and left.

On the way into town David wondered, even hoped, that his feeling toward this girl Jess might have faded, but as he sat in the shadows watching her every movement as if it were the first and most fantastic thing he had ever seen, he began to realise just how much trouble he was in. Poor Nikki, he didn't want to hurt her, but then, damn it, what about Steve Wilcox and what she did with him in the shower? And where was their relationship going anyway? He didn't know, only that later, when Jess caught sight of him sitting alone in the dark watching her and smiled, his heart started to flutter and it didn't matter any more.

'You like it?' Jess asked.

'Sure,' he said. 'It was great. You guys can really make those things spin, and you made a bit of money too.' After they had finished spinning the fire pois they had held a hat out for donations.

'Yep. Fifty bucks each. Not bad for half an hour's work.'

'And you guys do this every night?'

'Yeah, we've been doing it two years now, though it seems like only two days. You climb into your own little time warp here, I guess, and you don't want to get out.'

'Is this where you grew up?'

She laughed. 'No. I grew up in a tiny little town down in Victoria.'

'Tiny?'

'Yeah, it was a truck stop mostly, on the highway. My mum and dad ran a diner down there for all the truckers.'

'Did you like it?'

'Yeah, it was a fun place to grow up. Not much to do there when you get older, though. It was good to leave, and really good to come here.'

'You like living in Byron Bay?'

'It's easy. There's magic here, there really is.'

And she was right. It took a couple of days but he did begin to understand what she meant. They had sat in the park till late that night. It was so comfortable there was no real reason to leave. She asked about his art and was actually seriously interested and enthusiastic, telling him that she'd love to see him work. She also told him that she knew a guy who might be willing to share his studio. He lived on a small community just out of town where she spent a lot of time.

The next day he spent having a look around the Shannon markets while Nikki swam at the beach. When she said she wanted to go to the movies that night he lied, said he didn't want to spend the money, and went and spent the time with Jess instead. This went on for four or five days and, as Jess had said, he really did begin to feel the magic of the place. Days became hours, hours became minutes. He wasn't really doing anything, and he sure wasn't making any money, but nothing seemed to matter except the little things – what to have for dinner and how to escape spending time with Nikki to spend more time with Jess.

But on about the fifth or sixth day, after a rather shocking visit to the ATM where he learnt he had only eighty dollars left, he decided it was time to get to work. First things first. He took Jess up on her offer and arranged to meet her friend Justin.

Justin was an interesting character, one of the bay's most successful commercial artists. He was a bit older than David and a very different kind of painter. His work was more abstract and surreal. He was friendly enough, though, and opened his whole studio up to David, telling him to use whatever he wanted. David smiled. The studio was great. Built in an old attic above a barn at the front of a small organic farming community about half an hour's walk past the Arts Factory, it had all the equipment and space he could want and more. He knew what he wanted to paint too, although he didn't tell anyone, except Jess, who to his delight seemed as keen to be with him as he was to be with her. She was happy just to be near him while he painted, which he begun to do on the morning of his seventh day in Byron Bay.

David didn't get worried about Nikki until the tenth day. He hadn't made any sexual contact with Jess yet and even though he hadn't really told Nikki about her, the deception still seemed only mildly dishonest. But in the last few days Jess had become very touchy feely and David knew that if he did not answer her advances then sooner or later they would stop and he sure as hell didn't want that. He would have to tell Nikki it was over. He waited until Jess left to do her fire show that night then made his way down to the Arts Factory. But when he opened the tent and lit the candle he discovered a note where her pack had been.

'David – Frank, Stu and Rach were heading up to Cairns for a couple of weeks and they offered me a lift. Good luck with your painting, maybe I will be back in time for your big opening. Be well XXXX Nikki.'

David sat for a while in the dark, then walked out of the Arts Factory, into town and right up to Jess in the park, where he took her by the hand, led her down to the beach and made passionate love to her on the sand.

In the weeks that followed, David moved out of the Arts Factory and started sleeping on a mattress on the studio floor with Jess. He painted during the day, then watched Jess and her two friends, Mary and Karen, do their fire show in the evenings. Then he and Jess usually spent a couple of hours walking around town and the beach, watching the buskers and the waves before heading back to the studio where they would get naked, talk and make love until early morning. Jess was so easy to be around, so calm and relaxed. With Nikki he had always felt he had to meet certain expectations, but Jess enjoyed whatever happened. This was easy. Simple. He liked her and she liked him and they wanted to be together, so they were. He had nearly finished eight pieces of what he hoped to be a ten-piece exhibition and if they sold he would be able to pay Nikki back almost all the money he owed her. He had never intended to cheat her. He did not love her any more, that was clear, but he still liked and respected her and didn't want to cause her any harm.

'What are you thinking about?' Jess asked the night before Mullumbimby markets, after they had made love and he lay on his back staring up at the ceiling.

'Us.' There was a silence. His heart was missing beats. This was what had been on his mind. This was the block in his thinking. Jess was fantastic, but she was a bit of a drifter. Like a tumbleweed she moved around and maybe he was just a pole she had got stuck to, maybe all this was temporary for her. Sure, she might say this or that, lovers always do, but it doesn't always mean ...

'Us?' She looked away.

'I'm sorry.' Why had he said anything?

'No. No it's okay. I like you David, I do. And I think we should talk about this. Why not? What would you like to happen?'

Her directness surprised him, but he thought about it honestly for a moment. 'I'm not sure. I like you and I like it here. I'm happier here with you than I think I've ever been. I can paint and we always seem to have something to eat. In the city there's more people, more action, but it's like a big game and you need heaps of money to play it. I always thought that in London if you stopped working and paying your bills you'd be chucked in jail the same day, but here you feel free of all that somehow. You don't have to pay to be alive, everything is here and it's for everybody.'

'Everything?' She looked at him more seriously. She was right, too. There had been a but in his voice.

'No, not everything.'

'What's missing?'

'Change.'

'In Byron Bay?'

'Yes. Things are good here, they're easy, but it can't last forever, I can't ... one day ... I ...'

'Shush.' She raised a finger to his lips. 'I know you can't stay here forever, I wouldn't expect you to. You're ambitious, there are things you must see and do.'

'And you, what about you?' he asked.

'I'm not sure.'

'You don't like me.'

She turned around suddenly and grabbed his shoulder, her eyes ablaze with conviction. 'No David, I love you and I do want to be with you.'

'Really?' He was a little shocked, and very relieved.

She laughed. 'Yeah, really.'

Their eyes locked again and this time they kissed.

'So you'll come with me then?' he asked.

'But where would we go?' she asked with a chuckle, and the mood was suddenly playful again.

'I don't know, England maybe, or New Zealand.'

'But how? I have no money, I can't do anything. I have the fire show but that's all, and I couldn't just do that anywhere.'

'It doesn't matter. We would find a way. That you want to come, that you want to be with me, that's what matters.'

'And you wouldn't leave me for the next girl who smiles at you?' she asked.

David looked at her. 'What do you mean?' There was another silence. 'Nikki?' They hadn't discussed her but obviously Jess had felt her presence in his thoughts.

'You haven't told her about us yet, have you?'
'No.'
'And are you going to?'
'Yes, of course.'
'When?'
'As soon as she gets back.'
'Where is she?'
'She went up north for a few weeks with some people she met at the Arts Factory, she'll be back soon.'
'And then?'
'Then I'll tell her.'

Karen and Mary woke them up at six and in the early morning light they loaded David's paintings carefully into the boot of her car and headed out onto the road to Mullumbimby. The market started at nine. David was nervous. So much depended on how things went today. His paintings were good, and well priced for their quality, but that didn't mean anything if people didn't want to buy them. And no one knew who he was. Maybe he should have told the radio what he was doing, or the paper, drummed up some publicity. In a town this size it wouldn't have been hard.

They got to the site just after seven. Jess, Karen and Mary set up their stall right beside his, then crowded around as he got ready to pull back the white sheets and reveal his hard work, the finely detailed portraits of scenes from everyday Byron Bay life. 'The collection,' he told them, 'is called "Timelessness".' One of the paintings was of two Aborigines, a man and a woman, arguing in the park; another showed a strange, transient figure waiting in the shadow of the train station with a wet roll-your-own in one hand and a bottle in a brown paper bag in the other. It was raining and you could see a train in the deep background disappearing into the distance. The one beside that was of two businessmen shaking hands on the street. Behind them on one side was an empty shop with a small sign in the middle of the window that said, 'Coming soon, big business'; on the other was a brand-new black BMW. Both of the men looked rich, but one of them, the one receiving a briefcase from the other, had a tie-died T-shirt under his suit. All his portraits were taken from photos. Another painting was of Byron Bay seen from the lighthouse; another showed a statue busker, a young woman painted in white who blinked and blew kisses when you put money in her basket. Another was of a Kombi van parked outside the Arts Factory. The last depicted two men, one clearly a local and the other a tourist, exchanging money for drugs in the park where David had first seen Jess.

'They're great, David. You have a gift,' Karen said. 'And if you don't sell them it will only be because people don't have enough money to buy them, not because they don't like them.'

'You think the prices are too high?' David asked quickly.

'Maybe. As I said, it's nothing about your work, its great, and worth all of that if not more, but people here don't have much money. Two or three hundred dollars is a lot to come up with.' David thought about this for a while then decided to see how the day went. If nothing sold in the first couple of hours maybe he would lower the prices then.

After Karen and Mary had left, David took one of the front paintings off its easel and put it on the ground, revealing another covered painting behind it. Jess turned and looked at him. She counted the other paintings, then looked at him again, her face alive with curiosity.

'You said there were ten, but I've only seen nine, so that must be the tenth. But what is it?' He did not answer. 'David, tell me ... tell me.' Her voice was serious, but she was also smiling, enjoying the mystery. 'I don't know how you put that past me. I should have known. All that time ...' She stepped forward, he stepped back. They both laughed.

'Maybe I should just put it away,' he joked, putting it behind him.

'Don't you dare,' she said, grabbing a corner of the frame.

'All right, all right.' He turned it around.

'Wow!' she exclaimed, taking a step back from the painting.

'Is it okay?' he asked.

'It's beautiful, it's great ... it's ...'

'You don't mind if I sell it then? I mean, I know I should have asked you first and I'll understand if ...'

'Of course you can sell it,' she said. 'It's fantastic.'

He smiled. It was dangerous to paint people when they didn't know, but she had looked so damn beautiful lying there he couldn't resist. He had sketched her one night when she lay naked on the bed, her sandy brown hair and yellow skin pinched red by the sun contrasting fantastically with the white sheet. It was flat and silent and lifeless and she was so curvy and animated and full of life he could almost feel her pulse from across the bed. In the top right corner of the painting was written, not timelessness, but rather 'when time stopped'. Jess turned around and kissed him.

'It can go at the front,' he said, lifting it up and placing it gently on the easel. 'To bring the punters in.'

'And how much am I worth?' She asked.

'I'm not sure. I've decided not to put a price on you and just see what kind of offers I get.'

David sold the first painting in the first ten minutes for three hundred and fifty dollars to a farmer's wife. It was the one from the lighthouse, she said she liked it because it reminded her of something her granddad had told her from the days when he first moved to the area. The second one, of a woman and child in the surf, went for three hundred in the same hour. If it kept on like this then everything would be just fine. But it didn't. There were too many people and too many other things to buy. A few other people come and asked about the naked painting and he was always amused to see Jess looking up from the next stall when they did, but no one made an offer or even really looked at any of the others and by four o'clock he was beginning to get worried.

'You were asking too much,' another stall holder told him, an old man who appeared quite pleased about it. 'If you'd asked just one hundred then you might have sold something.' But David didn't agree. He had sold two paintings and he would have had to sell seven to make as much money if he'd sold them for one hundred. Jess agreed with him and said she didn't like 'old Harold' much and that he always thought he knew everything. But both she and David liked what happened next even less.

When David was returning from a trip to the toilet about five o'clock as the market seemed to be finishing up he saw Nikki standing in front of his stall looking at the painting of Jess. He walked up and stopped just a few metres behind her.

'Pretty girl,' she said, without turning around. 'You have sex with her?'

He stepped back. What the hell could he say? What could he tell her? He had come up with some things that night when he was walking down to tell her, clichés mainly, but not even they were anywhere to be found now. And now he could feel Jess nearby. She had walked up and was standing behind him. Nikki turned and looked at David, then at Jess, then back at David. He had a feeling she might get violent, but instead a tear come into her eye.

'Okay,' she said. 'Okay.' And with no more explanation she turned and left.

David looked at Jess who looked back at him, then looked away. 'Are you going to go after her?' she asked. Yes, part of him wanted to go after Nikki. She was hurt, and he wanted to make her feel better. But was that really possible now? He could not be with her, he had to be where he belonged, where he was happy and that was with Jess. He could see now that Jess was upset too and that he needed to comfort and reassure her. He stepped forward and put his arms around her. 'It will be okay,' he told her. 'Everything will be okay.'

The next two days seemed to move with gruelling slowness. David didn't see Nikki. Jess had run into her in town and said she looked really sad, so she was still around. But of course she was – David owed her a shitload of money. He had six hundred dollars left from the markets and about five hundred coming in a week or two from Christina in London, and he could keep going to the markets too and maybe next week he would sell some more, so he would be okay and he could give her something. But money was important to her and he knew that she would not leave until she had all of it.

In the meantime he still slept in the studio with Jess, still ate and went for walks in the afternoons before she went into town to do her fire show. 'We can share that money,' she kept insisting, not really sure of why he was so down about it all, but he didn't want things to be that way. He could not take from one girl while he still owed money to another.

By the fifth night he felt a little better and decided to go into town with Jess to watch the fire show. He had been sitting there for about an hour when by chance he looked up and saw Nikki across the street. She was with some other people from the Arts Factory and they seemed to be walking between pubs. Nikki was wearing make-up and seemed to be having fun. Seeing her and knowing that she was at least a little bit happy made David feel slightly better too, and after the fire show he followed Jess down to the beach and they sat on the sand. A group had gathered down the beach a little way and were drumming under the full moon. A young woman standing up in the circle was singing, her voice standing out and carrying further than the other sounds. It was a Nina Simone song. David had heard on the radio that she had died that week.

'You okay?' Jess asked and David looked back at her and knew exactly what she was asking. She was asking if he had finished brooding over Nikki and was ready to get on with their life. And he had.

The Price of Living

YOU'RE IN THE fifth white house, on the fifth white street, in the fifth white neighbourhood, on the fifth side of town. And you like it. Sometimes. When the sun is out, or your wife is pretending to be happy and the neighbour's kid calls you 'sir', and the Sunday morning paper lands right outside your door. It's the good life, but not all the time. In fact most of the time you can't stand it, you despise it, hate it for everything it is and everything it's done to you.

You were cool once, different; a new person at the great table, ready to drink from your own, original-shaped cup. And yet the freedom years seemed too drawn out, and the cup was too heavy to lift, and you were convinced that you needed to change, to have all the things everyone else had. And it didn't take long to get them, either; just five months separated being homeless, single, unemployed from the mortgage, the wife, the financial success.

The Price of Living

Only now it seems it will take forever to get out of it.

And you want to. You stand in front of the window every night, your gaze lost in the dim and unassertive glow of suburbia, trying to figure out a way ... There has to be an answer, a solution. Everyone else must do it, too, and you half expect to see them, staring back at you from behind their own windows. Faces, eyes, mindless empty-hearted expressions in the night. If only you could talk to them, share the problem, help each other out instead of competing.

You have to get out of here, you have to. The quest follows you to bed every night, and keeps you awake long after your partner has gone to sleep. Eat, work, sleep, die. There has to be more, there has to be. And you do the maths, over and over again. Calculating the price of living. What it will cost to pay the mortgage and all the other bills, to bring up the kids, to take them to the football matches, put them through varsity, to keep them in the type of clothes that society will tell them they have to have.

And yet, if you look really hard, you can see a narrow surplus between your income and the bills, a slim chance to do and be all the wonderful things that you had imagined when you were staring down into that great cup, an opportunity for just a sip of that freedom they showed on all those glossy mortgage brochures. And yet it never does quite work out that way, does it? There's always a broken tooth or a flat tyre, some unexpected bill to snatch that money away. Still, you add and subtract, searching your mind for a solution as your eyes become heavy and the drone of the traffic on the highway five blocks over blends into one long shooshing sound, and the slow sleep of suburbia comes and gently takes everything else away.

Way Down Below

'So you're a city boy then, are you?'

'Yep, Auckland.'

'Auckland, eh? Went there once, prick of a place, people everywhere, all running round trying to make a buck more than the next bloke. A fella could find himself in trouble in a place like that a little too quickly for my liking.'

'Yeah, well, I guess that's why I left.'

'What, trouble? You'd better not be on the run, boy. We've got no room round here for crooks.'

'No, I meant I left 'cos I was sick of it.'

'Well, there's plenty of work in the Waikato. Why didn't you just go there?'

'Yeah, well, see, this guy picked me up, said he was going all the way to Dunedin, wanted me to hang out I guess, paid for me to get across on the ferry and everything. Then, when I got out, that lady at the shop told me you'd been looking for a worker.'

'It's a long way to come if anyone was looking for you, too, I bet.'

'Nah, I told you, I'm not on the run.'

'Not from the police?'

'Nah, man.'

'And you reckon you can do the work?'

'Yeah, I reckon I can give it a go.'

'Well, we'll see about that, but I'll tell you this right now: it's no city round here, and there are no free rides neither. If you work you'll get paid, and if you don't you won't be here long enough to complain. You got it?'

'Yeah, I got it.'

'And if you give me any trouble, any bullshit at all, I'll be ringing the Johns as quick as look at you, right?'

'Right. So you're giving me the job?'

'Now just hold on a minute, I'm not giving you nothing. You stick it for two weeks and we'll talk then. That should be long enough to see if you're cut out for it or not. The pay's three hundred bucks a week plus a room and three feeds.'

'Great. When can I start?'

'Tomorrow's as good as any. Where's the rest of your stuff? You leave it in town or something?'

'Nope, I've got it all here.'

'In there?'

'Yeah, I ain't got much. I left town in a bit of a hurry I guess.' Sam realised his mistake.

'You sure you're above board, boy? You'd better not be mucking me around. A bloke doesn't like to be mucked around. Straight up is what we are around here.'

'Suits me.'

'It better.' The farmer, who had introduced himself as Frank, paused for a moment, and gave Sam another good looking over. 'Right, well, I'll show you to your room then.'

Relieved, Sam followed Frank out of the kitchen at the front of the house where they had been talking, across the yard toward a small hut that looked like a converted hen house. He stood back as Frank opened the door, then looked inside.

'Well, this is it,' Frank announced with a thin, almost sarcastic, smile.

But Sam had seen worse. 'Choice, this is sweet as.'

'Right,' said the farmer, a little disappointed. 'I'll leave you to it then. Dinner will be in about an hour.'

Sam stood just inside until Frank was back in the house, then closed the door to take a better look at his new home. There wasn't much: a wire mattress on one side, a three-quarter bed with two broken legs, flanked by a wooden chair with three, and a borer-eaten set of drawers held up mostly by the other wall. There was a small window that looked out into the yard, and enough light to see the yellow water stains frosted into the off-white walls, and the black mud caked on the wooden floor. A naked bulb hung from the middle of the ceiling. Sam looked for the switch, and when the light came on he saw the most important thing, beside the bed. A power point! An hour, he thought, I can do heaps in an hour.

On the ground outside was a piece of timber with a flat edge, and a woolsack on top of a forty-gallon drum. Sam found a bucket, too, and he filled it three times, throwing the water into the room to loosen the mud. He then scraped it up with the piece of timber, until, after five more buckets, the floor was clean. Most of the water drained away though the floorboards and he soaked up the rest with some old towels from on top of another drum. He propped up the drawers with some boards, lined the compartments with newspaper and reinforced the bed with four concrete blocks. There was even an old mattress on the grass beside one of the sheds. As he dragged it in through the door, Sam wondered if

Frank was watching. Probably was – bet he was pretty impressed too.

Sam sat on the bed. It had almost been an hour. What else? Curtains! He thought for a moment, then looked in his bag and found the sarong Tracy had given him. It was perfect. colourful and everything. He pinned it up over the window, then unpacked the rest of his clothes into the drawers, laying his sleeping bag and pillow out on the bed before gently taking his most prized possession from the bottom of the pack. He checked it over carefully for cracks. None, thank God. He'd die if he broke it. It was the only thing his mother had left him. He put the little TV on top of the drawers, plugged it in and checked the reception. All the channels were okay. Yep, sweet. He turned it off again.

It was nearly time to go up to the house. A cigarette first? Yes. And a moment to think. What was the plan again? Why was he here?

Before leaving, Sam stood at the door to look over his handiwork. With the TV and his bag on the chair, his sleeping bag on the bed, the sarong in the window, it was as cosy and as homely as any room he'd ever lived in. He smiled proudly. It looked bloody good.

Sam hesitated at the door of the house. Should he knock? Something inside him said he should.

'Come in.' Frank was sitting at the table with a cup of tea. 'Make yourself at home out there, did you?'

'Yep.' Sam stared nervously at the old man. He didn't know what to say.

'Well, what are you waiting for? I ain't gonna bite you.'

'Ah ... okay, sorry.' Sam sat down and Frank filled a second cup from the pot, stirring in milk and sugar, but he didn't hand it to Sam.

'Well, come on. I'm not here to wait on you hand and foot. The cups are over there, beside the fridge.'

Sam sat back in the chair opposite Frank and poured himself a cup of tea. He usually drank coffee, but the sweet tea tasted pretty good. He drank most of the cup quickly, then slowed down before it was all gone. There were two pots and a frying pan with food in them on the table too, and Sam found it hard not to stare. It was a long walk out along that gravel road, and he hadn't eaten anything all day.

'You hungry? Well, don't be shy. If you're hungry, dig in. You don't have to wait.'

Sam wanted to, but something inside him told him to wait, that it could be a test. 'It's okay. I don't mind waiting.' Sam could feel himself being examined, and he hid his unsteady hands under the table. Frank seemed a little disappointed again, too, but Sam was determined to hold out.

'Righto.' Frank swallowed the last gulp of tea and reached forward to take the lid off the first pot. He dished himself up three potatoes, three sausages and two fried tomatoes. Sam waited until he'd finished, then did the same. He ate quickly, no longer caring if Frank was watching him or not.

'Hope you work as well as you eat,' said Frank, still chewing on a sausage. 'But go ahead, finish it if you want. This'll do me.' Sam hesitated. Would it be rude? Nah. He nodded his head, and without speaking he finished the rest of the food.

'Been a while since you had a proper feed, huh?'

'A while, yeah.'

'Well, it's like I said before, if you work well you'll eat well too.'

Sam was happy. He had a job, a place to live and a meal inside him. A good meal too, not chips from the shop or McDonald's, so he wouldn't be hungry again in half an hour. He sat back, feeling more comfortable than he had in a long time.

'Now, don't be getting too cosy, there's the dishes yet. Everything's done fair round here, and I did the cooking.'

Sam was unsettled again doing the dishes. He could feel Frank watching him from behind and it was as if his every move was being picked up, looked at, then inserted into some strange picture of himself forming behind Frank's eyes. When he'd finished he turned to see Frank sitting in the same seat with his glasses on reading a classic car magazine, and Sam wondered for a moment if he had really been watching him at all.

In his room Sam closed the door and sat on the bed. He wanted to be angry with Frank for being so blunt, but he couldn't be. People were always pretending to be comfortable around him when they weren't, when they were really frightened, of him, of his past, where he come from, what he might do. At least Frank was being honest about it. And even though he made himself out to be a hard ass, Sam had a strong feeling that he probably wasn't so bad. He'd given him a feed after all, a place to stay when he didn't really know him, and a job that paid three hundred bucks a week. That was about eight hundred in the city after accommodation and food, and a thousand if you had a car and liked going out in the weekends.

Leaning back against the wall with his feet up on the bed, smoking a cigarette, Sam thought of his friends in the city. What would they be up to? Tom, Paddy, Jim, Shorty? Tracy too. What would she be thinking? Maybe she'd be doing someone else already. Sleeping in their bed. Jim would make a play for her pretty quick. He was always dropping hints, and the others wouldn't be able to stop him either; he was such a cunning prick, they probably wouldn't even know. Maybe he could ring her in a week or two and find out. Maybe if things were good she could come down. He might have a car by then, and the old guy probably wouldn't mind having her around either.

After a while Sam turned the television on and got into his sleeping bag. It was only ten o'clock, a lot earlier than he usually went to bed, but it had been a long day and pretty soon he drifted off to sleep.

There was a tank, men with guns. Sam was running forward, the first man into enemy territory. People were being gunned down all around him. They lay dying on the ground. Some grabbed at his ankles as he passed, pain twisting their mangled bodies. Their cries filled the air. He wanted to help them, but he kept going, running, faster, faster. The man with the machine gun was behind a rock up ahead. Anger flooded Sam's brain. He had to stop him, kill him if he needed too. He was almost there. Fifty metres, thirty, twenty ... He raised his gun, he took aim. Ten metres, five, two. *Bang*! Something hit the top of Sam's helmet. Something hard, but it wasn't a bullet. He stopped. Things were changing. There was a rock on the ground. *Bang*, and another. The air was closing in. Everything was getting smaller. The helmet was lifting off his head, into the air above him. He looked up. Without the helmet the next rock would kill him. He wanted to scream, to run back with the others, but he was trapped, he couldn't move. He started grabbing madly at the air around him and parts of something he couldn't see filled his hands, something soft. It began to materialise around him. He opened his eyes as another rock landed on the tin roof above him and he recognised the farmer's voice coming from the front of the house. 'Rise and shine, sonny Jim.'

Sam looked at his watch. Five am! What? Bloody hell. The old guy must be bonkers. He put his head back down on the pillow. Maybe this wasn't his cup of tea after all. He closed his eyes. Dreams were coming back, nice ones too. Tracy was there, and another chick, and they were kissing. Sam smiled, why would he ...? *Bang*! This time the rock was bigger and its impact shocked Sam into full consciousness.

'Okay, all right,' he shouted. 'I'm getting up, I'm getting up.' The front door of the house shut and Sam sat up on the edge of the bed. What should he wear? What would they even be doing? He didn't have a clue. He had a pair of sneakers and trackpants, but they wouldn't do. His good jeans and boots? But what if he wanted to go out? Nah, there wasn't anywhere to go. Nothing in the town but a couple of shops, a garage and a pub, and he couldn't see himself going there in a hurry; it looked like a dump. He put on his jeans and boots and stepped outside. It didn't really matter. If he lasted just one week he'd have enough money to buy some more.

Frank met Sam by the front door. 'Here, these ought to fit.'

'Thanks.' Sam took the overalls and started putting them on.

'You know how to drive a tractor?'

'Ah ...?'

'Well, you know how to drive a car, don't you?'

'Yep, had one last year. A '67 Falcon GT, had a V8 engine in it and everything.'

'Really, well if you can drive one of those, you'll get the hang of this pretty quick.' For a second there was something different in the old man's voice. '67 GTs were pretty rare and Frank was interested in cars. 'Well, come on then, we haven't got all day.' Sam turned around, still fumbling with the zip on the overalls, and climbed up to the seat of the tractor. Frank came in the other door and stood in the space behind. 'Right, now there's eight gears here and they can all be split with this lever, which means there's sixteen. But it's not like a car, you choose which one you want before you start. Got it?'

'Yep.'

'Now this is the high and low ratio lever.'

'So there's thirty-two gears?'

'No, there's sixteen.'

'But ...?'

'Don't worry about that now, it doesn't matter. Here, look, you choose high or low ratio before you start, then put it in the gear you want – fourth will do for now – then you select the revs. To get down to the paddock you'll need about twelve hundred, and then you let out the clutch, see. Simple.'

'Sweet.' Sam let out the clutch and the tractor started with a jump, the front wheels lifting right off the ground.

'Easy I said, easy.'

'Should I try it again?'

'No, just keep on going, out that way.'

Sam drove the tractor out the gate and onto the road, trying hard not to smile. He'd never driven anything so high off the ground before, or even been in anything so expensive. He read in a magazine once that tractors like that were worth about four hundred thousand bucks

'Right – clutch, brakes.' They stopped about a kilometre down the road and Frank got out of the tractor to open the gate, waving Sam in. The take-off was jumpy again and Sam caught Frank shaking his head. In the paddock Frank directed him to another piece of machinery. 'Right, now back in here.'

Frank showed Sam over the workings of the machinery. How to put it on and take it off, how to lift it at the end of the rows from the cab of the tractor and lower it again at the start of the next one. Sam listened carefully, visualising each action, intent on getting it right.

Frank stood in the cab right behind Sam most of the morning, offering advice, correcting his mistakes, but Sam was getting the hang of it pretty fast and after their morning cup of tea, which Frank produced from behind the seat of the tractor, he said he'd have to leave him alone. He had some business at the white house down the road a bit.

'The rest of the paddock should take you to lunch, then there's another paddock of potatoes across the road. I'll be back this afternoon and we'll see how you've got on then.'

There was a flutter of excitement in Sam's stomach, but he kept it from appearing on his face. The old man might get suspicious if he looked too keen. He waited until Frank had climbed the fence, then swallowed the last gulp of his tea and climbed back up into the tractor. Suddenly there seemed to be so much – so many levers and buttons in front of him, on the roof, on the floor. What was he meant to do, again? Turn the key. No, push that thing in first. No, yes, yes that was it. There it goes. Now the gears, the ratio, that lever, this one, sweet. Hydraulics? Got it. Yeah! Halfway down the row already. Who's the man! Check me out now, Trace, big green tractor. I'm a farmer, a farmer, man! Two rows, four rows, eight. Piece of cake. I'll be finished this paddock before lunch.'

When he'd finished the paddock Sam closed the gate behind him and parked the tractor on the side of the road. He ate the lunch Frank had left, then walked across the road to look over the second paddock. There were two. Two gates, two paddocks! Which one was he meant to do? He wasn't sure. They both looked the same. Did it matter? No, of course it didn't, and he'd do both before the old man got back if he could anyway. That'd impress the old bugger. Yeah, he opened the gate to the paddock on the right and drove the tractor in.

Sam had finished most of the paddock when he caught sight of Frank walking back along the road. He had something on his face that Sam had not seen yet, and Sam almost had to look twice to make sure it was the same man. Yeah, he's stoked I've started on the second paddock, Sam thought happily, concentrating even harder than before. It's just a pity I haven't started on the third. And yet, at the end of the row, when he looked back and Frank was closer, the smile had gone.

Frank gave Sam the rest of the day off. He hadn't said anything about Sam's efforts, no words of praise or encouragement. Back in the yard the old man disappeared into the house and shut the door without saying a word.

There was still heaps of daylight left. Maybe he could go into town or something. The old man might have a bike he could use. He still had ten bucks left and there'd be people there. He could find someone to talk to. Some of these farmers had to have daughters, and it'd be nice to talk to a chick. Tracy wouldn't mind either, not if they just talked.

Taking a deep breath, Sam walked across the yard to knock on the closed door.

He recognised Frank's condition straight away. He was drunk.

'Ah, Frank, you got something I could use to get to town? A push bike or something maybe?'

'Bottom shed.' Sam turned to see where Frank was pointing, and when he turned back the door was shut.

Motor bikes, push bikes, lawn mowers, a go cart – falling over each other, collecting dust. Some of it was really old, and really valuable too, Sam guessed, recognising some of the bike badges from a magazine he'd flicked through a couple of times at his uncle's house. Maybe he could ask Frank about the go-cart one day, if the moment came. He'd always wanted to drive one. He looked around for a push bike. There was a red one hanging on the wall that looked like it might go. He took it down and out into the yard, testing the tyres and the brakes before collecting his stuff: wallet, the ten bucks, jacket, durries. Sam was feeling a bit tired again. Maybe he could have a smoke before he left, put his feet up.

Sam woke to the sound of a large engine revving in the yard outside his room. He lay dazed for a moment, then rushed over to the window just in time to see Frank pull out in a white Falcon just a couple of years different from the one he'd had in the city. 'But you're drunk, you're drunk.' Sam started out the door to stop him but it was too late. He watched the tail lights flash between the trees, then disappear as the car rounded the corner down the road.

How long had he slept? Four hours! He was hungry now, too. Really hungry. He tried the door to the house. It was locked. Now he'd have to go into town, even if it was dark. He couldn't go the night without food. Hadn't the old man seen his bike outside the hut? Didn't he know that he hadn't had anything to eat? Nah, he was pissed, he probably wouldn't have even thought of it. 'Bloody idiot. Three feeds a day, my ass.'

Riding on the gravel was hard and took a lot of getting used to. He had to stop a few times when he got caught in the ruts, and with no lights they were hard to see. The chain came off twice, too, but both times Sam managed to put it back on by feel without loosing his cool. It got easier when he got to the tarseal, and easier still with the lights of the main road leading into town.

At the fish and chip shop Sam talked to the owner while he waited, then sat on a chair out the front of the shop drinking a can of Coke and smoking a cigarette.

The old man's car was parked outside the pub down the road. He'd be pissed as anything by now, thought Sam, serve him right for leaving me with no food. I hope he ... Sam stopped. What was he thinking? What did it matter if the old guy had got drunk? He wasn't his father. Sam finished the cigarette. Maybe he should go down there and see if Frank wanted a ride home or something. Yeah, why not? He'd given him a job after all.

Sam put his bike against the wall at the back door of the pub. A long corridor led him to the bar's entrance, and he stopped before opening the door. There were only a few voices inside and he waited to hear Frank's. 'Hey Coxie, listen to this. Frank's got this kid from the city working for him. Come on Frank, tell us what he did again.'

'He, ah, he dug the wrong paddock with the tra ... tractor.' Frank's voice sounded stunted, like he was out of breath or something.

'Yeah, that's right Coxie, he dug the carrots. He was meant to be doin' the spuds ... cost Frankie boy five thousand bucks.' The stranger's voice was followed by roars of laughter, then a loud thud.

Why hadn't the old man told him he'd got it wrong? Sam turned around, embarrassed. He wanted to leave. Leave the old man there and then, leave the farm, the stupid country and all the stupid people in it. 'Shit!' Why hadn't he just told him? He began to walk back down the corridor, but stopped again. The old guy had got drunk, drove into town, mouthed off to his mates about him, made a bit of an ass of himself, but he hadn't fired him. He hadn't fired him! That meant something. Sam turned around and burst into the bar.

Frank had fallen off his chair and was sitting on the floor, trying to get up, while his mates stood around, still laughing. Not one of them was trying to help him up. Now Sam was angry, and he didn't care how many of them there were, or if it was their territory. They could stick it. He walked over and began helping Frank up off the floor.

'Hey, who's this cunt?' one of them asked.

'I know,' said another. 'It's the carrot boy. Hey carrot boy, what do you think you're doing there?'

'I'm helping him up ...' replied Sam, turning to see a small round man with big eyes standing beside the person he presumed to be Coxie. He could take him out easy enough, and Coxie too if he got fired up enough , but he was there to pick Frank up, not to get into a fight. '... And I'm driving him home.' He continued, 'Here Frank, you got your keys?'

'In his car. I don't know if we can let him do that, can we boys? You might steal it, swap it for some carrots or something. We don't trust no one we don't know round here, and no one we don't like neither.'

Sam noted the change in the round man's tone, but he didn't care. If he had to fight he would. He wasn't scared.

'Here, wait boy, where you going?'

'I told you, I'm driving him home.'

'Hang on, carrot man.' Coxie stood forward and the round man walked behind Sam, nodding his head.

'Hey, hey,' said Coxie. 'Frankie, you want him driving your car?'

There was a moment of silence in the bar, until Frank finally managed to raise his head. 'It's okay, Coxie, he'll be all right.'

And with that the aggression dropped out of the two men's postures. 'Righto then, kid. We'll let you go this time. You enjoy those carrots now. Reckon Frankie will have you eatin' a few.' They laughed again.

'What about your car?' yelled the woman from behind the bar.

'He ain't got no car,' whispered the round man quietly almost into Sam's face as he approached the door. 'Have you, carrot boy?' Sam stopped beside him. He wanted to hit him – he could, the anger was there. The whole bar waited, and then, from under his shoulder, Frank lifted up his head again. 'Don't worry about him. That's just Smithie. He still pees his pants, has to wear nappies on the tractor.' The round man's face turned red and the whole bar roared with laughter again.

Sam put Frank in the back seat of the car. 'Stupid old git,' he said, smiling. 'Fuckin' should steal your car.' He put the bike in the boot carefully and drove them back to the farm. On the way Frank woke up a little and started mumbling something about a girl named Maria whose husband was coming back soon. Sam couldn't understand all of it.

The next few weeks passed quickly. Frank woke Sam up every morning at the same time; they'd have breakfast, and then go out and work until five or six, depending on what they were doing. Frank hadn't been out drinking since that first day, and neither of them had talked about what had happened. They had dinner together each night, and then talked, sometimes for hours, at the kitchen table. Frank knew heaps about cars, and a couple of times Sam even talked about the Falcon he'd had in the city. Sam asked him about the motor bikes, the go-cart, and once Frank even let him take his Falcon into town to get them dinner. It wasn't until later that night, when he was in bed, that Sam realised he hadn't once thought about stealing it. It would have been the perfect opportunity, too. He could have been halfway to the city before Frank realised he'd gone. He could have crossed on the ferry overnight and sold it for cash in Auckland the next day. They paid good money for cars like that, and the old man might not even dob him in. But what was the point? He'd already saved more than six hundred bucks, and it was his money, no one could take it away. And next week he'd have almost a thousand.

Over the weeks Sam also learned more about the Maria woman he'd heard Frank mumbling about on the way back from the pub. She lived in the white house down the road which Frank had visited every day since Sam had arrived. Frank didn't talk about her much, but Sam knew when he was thinking about her. Something came over the old man's face, a sparkle danced in his eyes. He was happy. They'd been together for years, it seemed, but she had a husband. Some guy in the city called Brian she'd been forced to marry to keep the estate or something. She ran the farm, the biggest in the district. She had heaps of workers, and a couple of times, when they were really busy, Frank and Sam went over to give them a hand. Maria was really nice, and Sam even asked Frank why he didn't just marry her at once, and to hell with the money. But Frank never really answered, he just laughed and said, 'If only life were so simple.' Sam loved seeing them together, though. Frank was much less serious, and laughed heaps when Maria was around.

Frank had become a lot more friendly with Sam too. One Friday night, after they had worked late, they went into town to get fish and chips and Frank even took Sam across to the pub to buy him a beer. Sam was a little nervous at first because Frank's mates still looked at him a bit funny, but they were all right once he'd talked to them with Frank around. Coxie even bought him a beer to clear the air. Sam knew a couple of others in the bar too, younger people from Maria's farm, and he had a couple of games of pool with them before Frank drove them home.

Then one night, Sam was woken up by a less familiar sound. He looked at his watch. Half past three – it was too early, even for Frank. He stumbled out of bed and turned on the light. Now there was no mistaking it. The banging wasn't rocks on the roof. It was someone at the door.

'Who is it?'

'Guess.'

Sam could hardly believe his ears. 'Tracy? Tracy! How the hell ...?'

'You've got my sarong in the window, silly.'

'But how did you get here?'

'What, ain't you pleased to see me?'

'Nah, yeah, course, come here.' Sam shut the door and wrapped his arms around her. 'Hey, it's cold. Here, jump into bed, it'll warm you up.' Sam tucked the open sleeping bag up tightly around her.

'You gonna get in too?'

'You want me to?'

'Yeah, of course, where else are you gonna sleep?'

'True.' Sam climbed into bed beside her.

'You miss me, Sammy?'

'Yeah, been thinking about you heaps.'

'You been with anyone else?'

'Nope, but there's this one girl who's been looking at me a bit funny lately. Her name's Daisy.'

'She sounds like a cow.'

'She is.'

'Funny.'

'Yeah. You?'

'What.'

'Been with anyone else?'

'Nah, stupid. Been hanging out though, that's why I come.

Took me a week to get down here. Hitched. Met some crazy people too. This one couple what took me home, tried to get it on.'

'What, both of them?'

'Yeah.'

'And you didn't?'

'Nah, the girl was okay, but the guy was real yuck, real sleazy and stuff. I had a bit of a smooch up with her when he went to bed, but that was all. Couldn't stop thinking about you.'

'So you ain't been with no guys?'

'Nope.'

'And you come all this way to see me?'

'Yep.'

'Wow!'

'Yeah, well, ain't you gonna kiss me then? A girl's come a long way.'

Sam smiled and pulled her close to him, kissing her first on the forehead, then on the lips. When she was warm again he began kissing down her neck. A thin glaze came over her eyes and she began to moan quietly as he started on her breasts. Sam stopped and looked up into her eyes.

'What is it? What's the matter?'

'Nothing, nothing. It's just good to see you, that's all.'

She smiled. 'Yeah, it's good to see you too, Sammy.'

After they made love she lay beside him with her head on his chest.

'So why did you leave, Sammy?'

He thought for a moment. ''Cos I had to, I guess.'

'Why did you have to?'

'I was sick of it.'

'Sick of what?'

'Of everything, not having any money, no decent place to live, no car, everything ... And then one day I was talking to this guy in the pub and he says to me, "Well, if you're so sick of it why don't you just leave? Get out of it for a while. Go live on a farm or something." He told me there was heaps of work, and heaps of ways to make a buck too if you knew what to take. So I thought yeah, bugger it, why not?'

'Were you sick of me too, Sammy?'

'I won't lie to you, Trace. It sucked not ever having any money to give you. Watching you walk round those second-hand shops and that, stealing food from the supermarket. It made me feel pretty stink sometimes. But, nah, I wasn't ever sick of you. I love you. I just wanted to make things better, that's all. I was going to come back and pick you up when I got it together, in a new car and that, buy you some new clothes, take you around the Coromandel or something, then bugger off overseas.'

'Were you gonna take me?'

'Yeah, course, if you wanted to go.'

'Is that the truth, Sammy?'

'Yeah Trace, course it's the truth.'

'So you didn't run out on me then?'

'No way.'

'Sweet.'

Not long after Tracy went to sleep, Sam got up to have breakfast with Frank. He ate nervously. He didn't know how to tell him that Tracy had arrived, especially since Frank had been in a funny mood the last day or two. He seemed pretty stressed. Maybe it was unfair to tell him. Nah, he had to. Frank would see Tracy anyway and it would be better if it came from Sam. Frank wasn't the type of guy who liked surprises.

'Frank. There's this girl I know from the city. We've been going out for a while and ... well ... I didn't really expect her to or nothing, but she turned up last night. She wants to stay for a bit ... I would pay for her food and everything.'

'Huh?'

'Is it okay if she hangs round for a bit? I mean, she's real nice and everything.'

Frank shrugged his shoulders indifferently, which was, Sam decided, as good an answer as he could expect.

'Frank, you okay? You been a bit quiet lately.'

'Huh?' Frank shifted uncomfortably, still not looking at Sam.

'You've been real quiet lately.'

'Huh?'

Sam watched him. He seemed to be in a dream, some kind of pain. Could the old man be losing his marbles? He didn't seem like the type.

Frank eventually shook his head and looked up from the table, and Sam could see that his mind was returning. The old man looked at the clock, shook his head once more, and was back. He was Frank again.

'Yes, you're right, we'd better get going. It's getting on. We'll leave the door open so Tracy can get in. And why don't you write her a note telling her to make herself at home? She can help herself to some breakfast and a shower if she wants. You know where the towels are. And we'll be working in the bottom paddock today too if you want to leave directions. Maybe she might like to walk down and say g'day.'

'Yep, right, great, thanks Frank. I really appreciate it.' But as Sam wrote the note, he couldn't help but be a little troubled by something. He could have been wrong, but he was pretty sure that he hadn't told Frank Tracy's name.

Tracy didn't come down to the paddock that morning, and Frank went off to the white house earlier than usual, leaving Sam alone on the tractor. He kept looking out for her, hoping to see her walking down the road or across the paddock. It would be cool if she came when he was working alone. She'd be impressed to see him driving the tractor and doing all the work by himself. But Frank arrived back about two and there was still no sign of her.

'Maybe she's still asleep?' Frank suggested. 'She's probably had rough couple of days.'

Sam watched Frank carefully. Something was going on, he could feel it. Was it Tracy? What would she be doing up at that house? Had she brought the trouble Frank had been so paranoid about? Maybe she had taken off, nicked something – the car maybe? What the hell was going on?

A bit after three, when they'd had their usual cup of tea and biscuits, Frank said he was heading up to the house. After he had left Sam really began to worry. Tracy was there because of him, he was responsible for her and, damn it, he didn't want to let Frank down. 'How could I have been so bloody stupid?' he said out loud, thumping the steering wheel in frustration. 'That stuff I told her last night, about knowing what to take. She probably thinks I'm here to rip the old guy off! Probably thinks she's doing me a favour. Damn it, why did I have to say that? Why?'

Sam's heart really beat hard about four o'clock, when, while turning the tractor around at the end of a row, he caught sight of a police car driving up the road. In a panic he started the next row, trying not to look. The car was checking him out. He could feel the eyes on his back. Were they going to stop? Were they going to take him in first? No, thank God, they had passed. He waited a moment, looked to make sure, then slammed on the brakes and ran across the paddock, and yes, there it was, the blue and white car, turning off the road and into Frank's yard.

Sam walked back across the paddock, got back into the tractor and rolled a cigarette. Was this to be his last day? The last time he drove the tractor, the last time he'd be free to do anything? He'd done nothing wrong himself, but he was still guilty: he had brought Tracy here.

An hour later Sam drove the tractor into the yard. Unless it was hidden around the back, the police car was gone. He thought about checking, but decided that, if they were watching, it might make him look more guilty. It was too late to run now anyway: they would have heard the tractor. He didn't look at the house, not yet, but took his overalls off outside his room and went in as if it were any other day. There was a lump in the bed, and for a moment Sam fantasised that it was Tracy. But the room was empty. He stepped back out into the yard and started toward the house, his heart beating a bit faster with every step. He took a deep breath at the door, and turned the handle.

They were both there, Frank in his normal place and Tracy where Sam usually sat. What was going on? They didn't look unhappy at all, they didn't even look upset. They were smiling, for Christ's sake, smiling and drinking beer. Sam stood staring, trying to understand.

'Hey Sam,' said Frank, 'how did you get on down in the paddock?'

'Sammy.' Tracy ran over and wrapped her arms around him. 'Did you have a good day?'

Frank's eyes changed. He looked suspicious. 'Sam, is something wrong? You look like you've seen a ghost.'

Tracy stood back. 'Yeah Sammy, you do look a bit pale. What is it?'

'There was a police car,' he stammered.

'Ah,' said Frank, relaxing his posture again. 'You needn't worry about that, me boy. There was a bit of an accident down the road, that's all.' Sam watched Frank. There was a glow in his eyes. He seemed happy.

'Was anyone hurt?'

'Just this guy from overseas,' Tracy began. 'He used to live down the road or something. Frank only met him once. Now come on Sammy, sit down. I've made us all a real nice dinner. Do you like what I've done with the place? Frank does!'

Sam looked around again. The house was tidier than he'd ever seen it, and once he was sitting down he began to feel a little better, too. 'Yeah, it looks good.'

'And I told Frank I wanted to cook yous something special for dinner too, so he let me take the car into town. Here, you want a beer? I bet you've had a hard day, out working and stuff. I'm so proud of you, Sammy.'

A little embarrassed, Sam looked over at Frank, who was smirking.

'You got yourself a tiger there, boy,' he joked.

Sam glanced up at Tracy. 'Yeah, yeah, I have.'

She smiled back at him, and his insides thawed out a little more.

'Okay then, Trace,' announced Frank, boyishly tapping his fork on his plate. 'Let's see what you can do.'

Sam smiled. Maybe he'd been worried about nothing. 'So what else did you do today?' he asked Tracy.

'Went for a walk down the road, picked some walnuts from this big old tree. Yeah, the country's okay once you get used to it a bit. It's real cool that no one is there to watch you and stuff. I walked down the road with my top off today. It felt real cool.'

Sam looked at Frank again, half expecting a reaction, but the old man actually gave Sam a wink of approval. And yet, well, this wasn't really the Tracy Sam knew, was it? The girl he knew was a bad ass bitch from the city, not some country bumpkin picking walnuts from a tree in the middle of a paddock. Could she have changed that much?

After dinner Tracy did the dishes and brought them another beer, chatting happily with Frank and flirting with Sam. Sam kept pinching himself to see if he was awake; he had never seen her so relaxed. It all seemed so odd. Under the guise of wanting a smoke he went back out to his room, and was halfway through the cigarette when Tracy came in.

'Got one of those for me?'

'Yeah.' He handed her the tobacco.

'What's up with you? What did you rush off for? There's beer and stuff. You like beer, and hanging out with Frank is fun, isn't it?'

Sam had never really thought of being with Frank as being fun.

'What, don't you want me here or something? I thought you ...'

'Nah, it's not that,' Sam replied. 'It's just weird, that's all.'

'Weird? What's weird?'

'Seeing you here, with Frank, doing housework, cooking and stuff.'

'Well, it's good here.'

'Good?'

'Yeah, there's stuff to do and that. Stuff to look forward to.'

'What stuff?'

'Well, this morning, I was thinking and I got this idea.'

'Yeah?'

'How much money you got?'

'About fifteen hundred bucks. Why?'

'Okay, great. I say we take that, the car, and a couple of other things and take off when the old man's away or something. We could get a really good head start and head off overseas or something, just me and you. What you reckon?'

'No way.'

'But I thought that's what you wanted?'

'Yeah, well maybe it was, but not now. I've got fifteen hundred bucks and if I wait a while I'll have two grand, then three, and then I can go with my own money. And besides, well, Frank's a bit of a grumpy old bugger at times, but he's okay.'

'Yeah, but you can't stay here forever, and we won't get far on two or three grand, not with both of us going. That wouldn't even pay for the tickets. Or maybe you're not planning to take me after all?'

'But what about Frank?'

'What about Frank, Sammy? You gone blind or something? He's

just a rich old git living on a farm. You gotta look after yourself in this world.'

'Yeah, well, I don't want to do anything, not now anyway, and if you want to stay you can't do anything either.'

'But ...'

'Nah, no buts. I like it here and I'm staying, at least until I can buy a new car or something. and if you want to stay too you gotta promise me you won't do anything stupid.' Tracy walked over and sat beside him on the bed. Sam took her hand in his and squeezed it. 'Come on Trace, you gotta promise me, okay?'

'But ...'

'Come on, you said yourself that the country's not that bad. Here, I'll give you some money. You can go into town tomorrow. I saw this clothing shop there, you can buy yourself some really nice stuff. Look, there's a hundred bucks, my treat.'

'Yeah, but ...'

'Ah, come on Trace, it won't be that bad. We're not going to be here forever and when we go we can leave in style for a change, in a new car that we've bought! Think what everyone will say in the city when we roll up. And we'd have worked for it too, me and you. Then we can go overseas. Come on, it'll be great.'

'You really want me to come?'

'Yeah, course, I wouldn't say it if I didn't mean it.'

'And can I come and visit you out on the tractor?'

'Yeah, of course.'

'And maybe they'll give me a job at the shop too. I know heaps about clothes, and the people I saw in that town sure don't. Maybe I could show them, make some money for us too.'

'Yeah, that's my girl.'

'All right then, I'll do it.'

'You promise?'

'Yeah, I promise.'

'Cool, now come here. I've been thinking about you all day.'

Tracy kept her promise. She didn't steal anything, not even clothes or money from the job she got at the clothing shop. She liked working there, too. People listened to her, looked up to her. All the local girls asked her for fashion advice, and some of them even started to dress like her. They asked her to their parties as well, which she went along to once or twice, coming home late, sometimes only just before Sam had to get up.

Things were going well for Sam too. He'd saved over two thousand dollars, the most money he'd ever had, and he and Frank were getting along better than ever. Frank hadn't gone to the funeral of Brian from down the road, but since then Maria had begun coming to the house a lot more, and a couple of times she even stayed the night. And she and Tracy seemed to get along okay too. Tracy said it was good to talk to an older woman because all the girls in the town were real young, 'and older people have some real good shit to say, if you listen.' Which surprised Sam because Tracy didn't usually listen to people much.

One day, about two months after Sam had first arrived, Frank left work especially early. Sam knew what he was doing anyway, so it wasn't a big deal, but when he got home, he found Frank, Maria and Tracy all looking at some travel brochures at the kitchen table. Tracy got up to greet him.

'Frank and Maria are going to go away for a few weeks,' she announced out loud before whispering, 'I think Frank's going to propose. Cool, huh?' into Sam's ear.

'Wow!' He looked over at Frank.

'Yeah, that's right, we're going to head up north. Maybe stay in the city for a bit.'

'But I didn't think you liked the city.'

'Yeah, well, maybe a bloke should take a better look around before he decides what he likes and what he doesn't.'

Sam sat down, a warm feeling circulating in his stomach. Even though it was indirect, what Frank had said was a compliment.

'When you going?'

'Tomorrow.'

'Tomorrow? But what about the farm?'

'You needn't worry about that, Sammy. I've written down exactly what has to be done.' Frank handed him a pad. 'I think you know how things work round here well enough now. You'll be fine on your own.' Sam finished reading the list, then looked back at Frank. 'See, you can handle it, can't you?'

'Yeah, well, I guess ...'

'Of course he can,' said Tracy. 'My Sammy can do anything.'

'Yeah, sweet.'

Frank and Maria weren't leaving until seven, but at six Sam found Frank sitting at the kitchen table.

'Thought you might have slept in,' he grinned.

'Nah, Sammy, habit's a hard thing to break. Here, have a cup of tea.' There was something strange about the old man. He looked almost as if he hadn't been to bed or something.

'Yeah, thanks. You looking forward to getting away?'

'Well, we'll see. Sam, there's something I want to tell you ...'

'You're getting married.'

'Yes, but there's something else ...'

Sam cut him off, not registering what Frank had said.

'That's really great, Frank. I'm real pleased for you. Maria is real choice.'

'Yeah.' Frank sat back in his seat, a troubled expression returning to his face. Was it fear?

They sat in silence for a while, until Frank looked up from his second cup of tea.

'Sam, can I ask you something?'

'Yeah.'

'Do you love Tracy?'

'Yeah, yeah I do, it's just that ...'

'That you don't trust her?'

'Yeah.'

'It's a cruel life sometimes, Sam, and there's some pretty mean people out there to, but some times you've just got to give people the benefit of the doubt. And you've got to hand it to the poor girl, she's been trying, she's really been making an effort. And it can't be easy for her – she's been dealt a pretty rough hand so far.'

'Yeah I know, I know.'

An hour later Sam and Tracy dropped Frank and Maria off in town to meet the bus. They would fly up north from Christchurch at ten thirty. Frank hadn't said anything about using the Falcon, and Tracy's enthusiasm about it on the way back to the farm made him nervous.

'Maybe we should just park it back in the shed when we get back. Only use it if we have to.'

'We'll use it to get food though, won't we? Frank left me some money.'

'Well, okay, for groceries, but that's all.'

Sam saw Tracy bike back up the road to the house about lunchtime. He wanted to stop the tractor and run over to her, apologise, but she was riding too fast. She must be pissed off. He wanted to go up to the house for lunch, but maybe he shouldn't, maybe she needed some time alone. He was getting hungry though, damn it. He left it a while longer, then stopped in the row and just before he turned the tractor off he caught sight of her climbing the fence.

He started forward again, pretending not to see her right until she got beside the tractor. She stopped and looked up at him. Her eyes were serious. Was she still mad? He watched her carefully. Her eyes didn't change. They stayed fixed on him as she reached down and started unbuttoning her shirt. She wasn't wearing a bra. She took off all her clothes and then reached down, still looking into Sam's eyes, to pick up the basket she'd brought with her. She then climbed up into the tractor, and putting a leg on either side of Sam, sat in his lap.

'Tracy, look, I'm sorry for what I said this morning I ...'

'Stop it, no talking.' Her voice was firm. 'I've just come to feed you, that's all.'

She put her hand into the bag and brought out a sandwich. Sam reached for it, but she stopped him. 'No, you don't understand. I've come to feed you.' She put the sandwich in his mouth and watched him chew, whispering things in his ears while he ate, dirty things – what they could do, what she wanted him to do to her. She kissed his neck, his ears, the sides of his mouth. Afterwards she took his hands and put them on her body, guiding them where she wanted them to go. 'That's it,' she cried. 'Keep doing that.' Sam went to undo his pants, but she stopped him. 'No, you've had your lunch, now you can wait till dinner.'

When Sam walked into the house that evening he could smell dinner, but there was no sign of Tracy. He called out.

'In here.' Her voice came from the lounge and Sam found her lying naked on the couch, still wet from the shower. 'I want you,' she said, her voice quiet but stronger than ever. Sam didn't hesitate.

Sam and Tracy made love a lot over the following week. They talked too, about travel – where they would go, who they might meet, how many times and in how many different places they could make love. The days passed quickly. They both got up in the morning, had breakfast, then went to work. Tracy finished at twelve and brought Sam's lunch to him on the tractor, and then he'd go back up to the house after five. Once she even stayed with him in the tractor all afternoon. Then on the tenth day, an envelope arrived in the mail.

Sam had worked late. He wanted to finish all the things on Frank's list early so he could maybe have a day or two off before he and Maria got home. When he got back to the house he found Tracy sitting at the table staring at the envelope.

'A courier delivered it about an hour ago,' she explained. 'And I waited for you.'

The envelope had urgent stickers all over it, but it was addressed to Frank.

'We have to open it,' Tracy burst out. 'It could be something important.'

Sam sat down for a while and thought. 'It does say urgent.'

'Yes.'

'Then yeah, maybe we should.' But he didn't move.

Tracy's eyes darted between him and the envelope. 'Well, come on then.'

'No, you do it.'

'Oh Sam, you're such a baby sometimes.' Tracy reached forward.

'Tracy, wait.'

'No Sam, we have to. Otherwise we're just not going to know.'

'Okay, damn it, open the stupid envelope.'

Tracy paused for a moment when she'd finished reading, then turned the page. Sam had never seen a person's expression change so quickly.

'Tracy what is it?'

'Sam.'

'What is it?'

'Sam, you're never going to guess what I am looking at.'

'What?'

'There's a letter here from some company. Says they're sorry the cancer treatment didn't work. They're offering Frank twenty thousand dollars worth of shares in the company – look, here are the certificates.'

Sam looked at her, then got up from the table.

'Sam, where the hell are you going? We're rich, Sammy, we're goddamn motherfuckin' rich!' But Sam closed the door behind him and walked out to his room to sit on his bed. It was the first time he'd cried since his mother had passed away. A few moments later Tracy's steps hurried toward the room. Sam wanted her to go away; he hated that she was so excited. 'Sam, what's up with you?

This is no time for tears.' Then her voice was soft again. 'Come on, what's up? You can tell me.' She sat down beside him and picked up his hand.

'The old guy's going to die!'

'Oh shit, Sammy, I'm sorry. I didn't even think, and after your mother and stuff. Sammy, I'm sorry. I'm sorry. I'm so stupid sometimes. Come here.' She held him in her arms and he wept for a long time.

Later Tracy convinced Sam to go up to the house to eat, and Sam sat deep in thought while she came and went from the table.

'I've got over two grand,' he finally announced. 'And I've nearly done everything that Frank wrote down on that list. What do you say we go for a drive to the city tomorrow? This guy told me there's an auction there. We can buy a car!'

'A car?'

'Yeah, we can get something real nice for two grand. Late model too, and we can both choose it. How's that sound?'

'And what about overseas, what about our future?'

'We'll talk about that later. For now let's just concentrate on getting the car.' Sam watched Tracy's response: she needed more. 'Frank and Maria aren't coming back for a couple of days. Trace, it's okay, we've got some time to think.'

'All right, damn it. We'll go to the city and buy the car then. I'll take the day off work.'

They didn't talk much on the way to the auction. They looked around the cars in silence, mostly, too, although their mood lifted a little when they got the one they wanted for seventeen hundred dollars. Sam fought hard to keep the shares out of his mind, but back on the farm they seemed to invade his every thought. Tracy was thinking about them too: he could see it in her eyes. But people would talk if two kids like them started splashing that kind of money around, wouldn't they? They'd start asking questions. And it was wrong to take it when it wasn't theirs.

'It's our future, Sam, our one chance at a normal bloody life,' Tracy burst out over lunch one day. 'What is it? What's wrong with you? Is it me? Don't you want a future with me – is that it?'

'No.'

'Then what is it?'

'I don't want a future like that.'

'Like what?'

'One made out of stolen money.'

'Ah come on, Sam, who are you really stealing from? The old guy's got heaps of money, Maria too, and all we've got is each other. Come on, they'd probably be happy for us. They probably wouldn't even call the cops. What would it matter to them?'

'It matters to me.'

'Why?'

'I don't know why, it just does.'

'So what are we going to do?'

'I don't know.'

'Well Sam, you'd better decide soon, because a chance like this won't come along again, not for the likes of me and you.'

Before the money they'd been happy, Sam thought. They hadn't even had sex since then.

'You need to know what you want, Sam. You need to make a choice. It's that simple.'

Sam woke up early next morning and got out of bed without waking Tracy. He made a cup of tea in the kitchen and sat at the table with a piece of paper and a pen.

Tracy
I know what I want and I'm sorry but it's not the money. But you're right, opportunities like this don't come along for people like me and you every day, so I want you to take it. Maybe we'll meet up again someday. I hope so. I know you don't believe me

sometimes, but I really do love you. Good luck Trace. No hard feelings. I really hope things go well for you.
I'll miss you heaps.
Love, Sam.

With a tear in his eye Sam left the share certificates and the keys to the new car beside the note and went out to start the tractor.

All morning he thought of Tracy. If she loved him she'd stay. She'd stay and be happy with him the way he was, the way he wanted to be. It was that simple. He didn't stop that day long enough to do anything more than roll cigarettes, not even when his face was soaked in tears. He wasn't Sam the dropout from South Auckland any more. He wasn't the Sam who everyone expected to be a thief, to do time, to end up nowhere. He was a man who'd passed up on twenty thousand bucks for his pride.

After Sam had pulled the tractor into the yard and taken off his overalls, he went into his room and closed the door. It was over now. He'd finished everything on the list, Frank and Maria were due back tomorrow and Tracy was gone. The window was bare. She had given him the sarong that time they hitched up north. He sank back into the bed and closed his eyes, remembering the way she had looked wearing it. She was so beautiful.

Sam only just began to stir when he heard someone come into the room. He opened his eyes. Was he dreaming? Tracy sat there, in the sarong. 'Tracy?'

'Yeah.'

'You're still here!' Sam looked at her suspiciously. 'Why are you still here?'

'Because you forgot to ask me something.'

'What?'

'You forgot to ask me what I wanted. I don't care about no money, I just want you. Why didn't you want me to stay, Sammy? Thought you were my man.'

And now it all made sense. He walked over to her, pulled her up off the chair and looked her straight in the eyes. 'Tracy.'

'What?'

'Look at me. I'm your man, and I love you. I'm so glad you stayed.'

It was raining the day they left the farm. Sam and Tracy packed their things into the car in silence, sad to be leaving. Frank and Maria were in the city, looking for a house now the property was for sale. As they pulled out of the gate, Sam stopped so Tracy could check the mail box one last time.

'There's one for you,' she said. 'It's Frank's handwriting.'

She opened it and read:

Sam,
Thanks for everything. Here's your last pay, and a little something to help you and Tracy on your way. Reckon you two are going to be just fine.
Good luck,
Frank and Maria.

'How much is it, Trace?'

She folded over the page. 'Twelve hundred bucks.'

'Good shit.' Sam turned to Tracy again. She had gone silent. 'What's wrong? Tracy, what is it?'

'There's another cheque.'

'A bonus? Wow, how much?'

'Sam, it's a cheque for twenty thousand bucks.'

You Lie

IT'S NOT THE first time you've slammed the door and left the house in the middle of the night, but that doesn't make it any easier. You're vaguely aware of your haste as the winter's air bites into your skin in the places where your clothes don't meet, but the sharpness doesn't cut nearly as deep as your lover's words, or your own.

You walk. A block passes. The words are still loud in your ears, penetrating and stinging your throbbing mind. You try to block them out, but it hurts, everything hurts. You try to think of something else, anything else, but it doesn't work.

Suddenly you remember some of the reasons why you fell in love with her. Her sense of self, an arrogance that intrigued you, the calm indifference that made her so easy to be around. The way she was always fashionably late, even to the most trivial things. And when she did arrive at the fish and chip shop, and later the altar, you always managed to forget why you were mad at her. Now you're not so sure.

More precise fragments pop into your head. The way she looked when she met your friends, your family. Her hair, her skin, her hands that touched no one else but you. You remember them squeezing your backside in the kitchen, when your mother wasn't looking, and how the whole thing felt so natural that you let your heart rest in what seemed like a safe place.

Another block has passed, and now, oddly, you can even manage a smile. You're almost calm. You become more aware of your surroundings. Your world seems different at night, almost smaller, but bigger in other ways, too. The voices in your head have gone, and you begin to realise the full magnitude of the silence. But then you hear something. A crash, a cry for help.

Nerves begin to churn your stomach. The noises are close – from one of the houses up the road, on the right. You stop, wondering what to do. Your better judgement tells you to go home – it's late, after three – but then the scream comes again, louder, more real, more urgent. You must help her.

You move swiftly, but not without caution. As you get closer the shouting becomes clearer. You're right outside the house now. There are no lights on at the front, but you see one down the side. You wait, wondering what to do. You want to be impulsive, you feel heroic, but you also want to live.

You can see the couple inside. There's an object in one of their hands and although you wish you didn't, you know what it is. The chill is back again. It crawls into your navel, around your sides. Winter seems to be embracing you, warning you, but you ignore it and, almost involuntarily, move toward the window. Closer and closer you get, and now you don't want to look, but you have to.

By manoeuvring closer to the fence and further away from the house, you assume safety, and yet you know that it will only take a single glance for you to be completely involved. You want to wake up. You wish you were asleep.

The woman has the knife to his throat, and you watch her threaten him. At first he doesn't seem to be intimidated, but you think you can see right through that lie and into his mind. Maybe it's because what he's yelling at her is so similar to what you were yelling at your lover less than half an hour ago.

Suddenly he grabs for the knife but she lifts it and it enters his throat just below his chin. Red blood pours from his white skin and he collapses on the floor. You step back, shocked and dazed. You wait, unsure of what to do next, unsure of what to think. The woman drops the knife to the floor, covers her mouth with her hands and steps away from the dying man. She seems as surprised as you are.

Now you have to leave. You run up the path, but stop. Your footsteps are too loud and you don't want anyone to know that you were there. You look around to see if anyone is watching you, but see nobody.

You've walked five or six blocks now and you need to sit down and rest. You've managed to fight the urge to run, but your mind has been racing all the way. You're scared, yet, strangely, a little calm too. For suddenly your problems seem trivial, less severe in comparison, almost acceptable. You're not so extreme, that couldn't happen to you. You look at your hands, and you can picture them wrapped around the knife, slashing too.

A police car has rounded a corner down the road and you watch nervously as it approaches. You want it to go away or to have seen it earlier and been able to hide, but it's too late. The car slows down, then stops.

The officer approaches and you manage to keep it together. You tell him that you just wanted to go out for a walk, that you're an insomniac suffering an especially bad night. And when he asks if you've seen anything out of the ordinary, you tell him that you haven't. You think to ask what he meant, but don't, and wonder, later, if he thought that unusual. But you dismiss it anyway. You've decided now that you want nothing further to do with this whole thing.

The officer leaves and you start for home.

You can feel your lover's warmth as you settle in on the opposite side of the bed, but the air is different. Although you've argued, and both of you have used some pretty sharp knives, they were only words and can be retracted without leaving fatal slashes. You think this, but you know it's wrong. One way or the other, one day you'll wake up alone, and you'll realise then that your steel tongue, when thrust hard enough in battle, cuts as deep as a knife.

High Flyer

THE LONG BLACK limousine pulled off the street in front of the building. The new concrete driveway was as smooth as marble and the tyres made a squeaking noise when they stopped beside the main entrance. A construction worker in an orange coat and yellow hat opened the door.

'Good morning, Mr Anderson.'

'Gary.' Kyle watched his father shake hands. 'Kyle, this is Gary. He built K1. Gary, this is Kyle. My son.'

'Hi Kyle, how are things down in the big smoke? Your father tells me you're doing pretty well.' Kyle looked between Gary and his father. Yeah, right. His father hadn't even asked about his grades in two years and he didn't know the first thing about what he was doing in Sydney. That was part of the problem.

Kyle looked up. The building went so high above them it almost hurt your neck to look up at it. The ground seemed to move under your feet when you did so, pulling you off balance. It seemed to tower directly over you as if it were falling over.

Kyle glanced back at Gary. 'You've been doing pretty well here too, eh? Wow!'

'Yep, tallest residential building in the world, as I guess you know. One hundred and twenty two floors.'

'And over one thousand apartments,' his father added.

'Wow,' Kyle said again. 'Wow.' But he was pretending now. In truth he didn't give two shits how many apartments the building had. Sure, he could do the mathematics. One thousand apartments selling at an average of six hundred thousand dollars each equals six hundred million dollars which, according to what he had read in the paper, was over four hundred million dollars more than it cost his father to build it, but why bother. It only made him feel bad. At university in Sydney he had met people whose parents paid more than three-quarters of their wages to live in houses pushed out of their price range by men like his father.

'Shall we go inside?' Gary asked.

They went in the main front door. The foyer was tall, ten storeys high maybe. The roof and exterior wall were made entirely of glass. In the middle two twenty-metre high sheets of glass were pressed together with water running down the middle in tiny streams that then fell three metres to a steel tray, making a pelting sound like rain on a window. Kyle liked this. He had read about it too. The designer was French and famous.

The floor around them was all white marble right up to the black reception area and beyond to the two small golden lift doors. They walked over and Gary pressed the up button. Kyle watched Gary carefully. He seemed like a nice guy, open, but he was nervous. His father had a way of making people feel nervous. Kyle didn't really know why. It was only a few lucky breaks that made him different. He certainly wasn't an exceptional man.

There was a ding and the lift doors opened. Gary stepped back.

He wasn't coming up. Kyle didn't like this. He didn't like being alone with his father. Still, maybe it was a good thing. Maybe it would give him one last chance. Gary smiled. The doors closed.

Inside the lift the doors were mirrored and Kyle looked at their reflections. His father was a good deal taller than him, and twice the build, with shiny black hair and pale white skin. His small dark grey eyes looked straight ahead. Kyle was short with blond hair and fair skin. His mother had been the same.

Kyle looked at the light panel: 34-35-36 ... They were going up fast. He didn't have much time. Perhaps he should try and tell him. It was too late to make things better, but it might make him understand what his son was about to do. He took a deep breath, turned a little ... No. He couldn't do it. It was too hard. And yet he had to, didn't he? Shit! 64-65-66 ... He took another breath. How had it come to this? How had it gone so far? If his mother had been alive she would have seen what was going on. He wouldn't even have had to tell her. And with her help, his father might have seen and understood too.

In all fairness he hadn't really hadn't had the chance to. The only time they had been together since her death was in the car on the way to the airport, and here. His father was never in the house, hardly ever in the country. Kyle had wondered if he was trying to hide something. Maybe he had started seeing other women. In a way, Kyle wouldn't have been angry if he had. It might have given them something to talk about, a rung on a ladder to climb out of his mother's grave where their relationship seemed to have been stuck for almost three years.

They used to talk. His father used to tell Kyle all about his plans, the things he was going to do. He had always liked that about his father, that he had made the most of his life. His mother had been the same in a different way. 72-73-74 ... Kyle turned again, but then swung back. This time he knew his father had seen him.

'Kyle, what is it?' Kyle looked down. He could feel his father's eyes looking at him in the reflection. They seemed so close, so intense. He couldn't look back at them. He waited instead for a sign of dismissal, a shift of weight maybe, but it didn't come. He could still feel the eyes. He looked up, met his father's gaze. 'What is it?' And Kyle wondered for just one moment if it really could be that easy, if he actually could just come right out and say it.

Dad, I hate my life. I hate society and capitalism and how no one cares about anyone else and I don't belong here and I feel trapped inside this body and it's horrible and I just can't take it any more. I feel so alone and sad and everything has been so dark since Mum died that I just want it to end. I can't relax. I can't think. I get so scared sometimes that I can hardly even breathe and every night I go to sleep and hope that in the morning I'll be better but I'm not and now I don't even want to wake up any more. I just want it all to end.

Kyle glanced back down at the panel ... 88–89–90. Time was running out. If he was going to tell him anything it was now or never.

'Something's been happening down in Sydney,' he began.

'Yes.'

'I ... I ...' Kyle hesitated.

His father looked away. What was the point? He wasn't interested and he wouldn't understand anyway. He would only think his son was weak for not being able to handle things better. In his world men were men and men didn't talk about how they felt. The moment had passed, anyway. It was gone. Shit. 112–113–114 ... Was it worth trying again? He took another breath. No, it was hopeless.

There was a ding and the doors opened. They were on the roof of the penthouse suite one hundred and twenty-three floors above the limousine, Gary, the Gold Coast and the smooth concrete entrance below. They stepped out of the elevator and walked through a glass door to a small white tiled courtyard. Kyle's father stood at the waist-high stainless steel rail, looking at the view. Kyle took a final long breath, one last look at his father, then jumped.

SOFT ASYLUM

KATIE STEPPED OUT of the phone box and looked again at the entry in the 'Workers on organic farms' book. *Happy Valley Community, PO Box 44, Byron Bay, cultivating organic crops and communal living. Work includes gardening, regenerating rainforest, cleaning, building, cooking and general maintenance. Vegetarian meals and places for up to 6 people in separate accommodation.* She'd rung at just the right time – one of their woofers was leaving that afternoon. Mel, the woman on the phone, had asked if she could cook, which was cool. She was looking forward to this, and Mel sounded nice. She put the book back in her bag, rolled herself a cigarette and sat down on the grass beside the car. What would it be like there? Could she imagine it? She'd seen a few photographs of communities, but the photographers don't show you how a place feels; if they did you wouldn't have to go there. Katie had tried to explain this to her mother lots of times, but she never really understood why her daughter had to go and experience these other places for herself. Her dad understood, of course, because he shared the same curiosity. Katie had always told her mum that she worried too much, but in truth, she concluded now with a little smile, it was comforting to know that her mum knew where she was and when she'd be back.

Byron Bay was quieter than she'd thought it would be. She remembered coming here for New Year's Eve when she was eighteen, and the now placid streets teeming then with young adults all getting it on. She'd seen another side of Byron Bay when she was even younger. She used to stop off there with her parents for ice cream on the way up to Brisbane to visit her aunty and cousins. Then there were hippyish people wearing wildly bright coloured clothes and big smiles. They all looked so happy. She had always wanted to go back there, to run away to Byron Bay and live like them, to be wild and naked and free. But by the time she was old enough, tourists and people with heaps of money had pretty much taken over the place and the town had got too expensive. Most of the wild people had either left or turned to selling drugs to make enough money to stay. It just didn't seem the same any more.

She drove slowly, staring out at the land when she could. She liked this part of the country. It was a shame that so many rich people had moved here first and forced the prices up. She imagined living in a house on a hill somewhere, doing a bit of work on a laptop maybe, shooting into town to pick up milk and bread, bumping into some of the locals, having a drink at the local pub, coming home when she'd had enough of the outside world.

A while later she stopped and looked at the map again. She'd passed the horseshoe turn and was now back beside the ocean again. If her calculations were correct the community must be in the valley right around the corner and probably only a few minutes drive away, which also meant that Potts Beach was just over there. Perfect. She parked the car, had a stretch, found her towel and started off over the sand dunes.

Katie stopped at the top of the sand dunes and looked out over the ocean. It wasn't what she had hoped for. There were too many rips to go swimming by herself, so she walked down the hill and looked for a quiet place to sit down instead. Maybe this time she could make the cigarette last.

What did she hope to gain from this time? She liked to have a goal before she started something new, something to work towards. Should it be to relax more? She'd been quite nervous and unsettled lately. No. She thought about it a while longer. What did she really want? She wanted peace. To be somewhere with people who didn't think she was weird. She was sick of being the outsider, never fitting in anywhere. Maybe this would be different. She stubbed the cigarette out in the sand. If things were different she would want to stay here for a while longer maybe, but it was too quiet and lonely for how she felt now.

Then, out of the corner of her eye, she saw a man walking up the beach in her direction. She felt her pulse quicken a little. She hadn't seen another human being since Byron Bay, and she couldn't help but be a little intimidated. She watched him for a moment. What were the rules in a situation like this? She sat down again and rolled another cigarette; at least if he saw her it would look like she was doing something.

The man was young, in his late twenties or early thirties. He wore light brown pants and a dark green long-sleeved T-shirt, both rumpled and a little scruffy. His brown hair was wavy and hung down over his collar. Thick wooden beads dangled from his neck. Was he from Happy Valley? He had to be, didn't he, dressed like that? Katie watched him more carefully as he got closer. She could see his face clearly now. He was quite attractive, really. A little mysterious and wild-looking too, but she liked that. When he was right in front of her on the beach he stopped, turned and looked out to sea, and suddenly the situation seemed a little strange. She breathed, relaxed a little. Everything was all right. She followed the man's gaze out to sea. Maybe he was looking for answers, just like her. After a while he turned, kept walking as Katie finished the cigarette, and climbed back up the sand dune. He was a little further down the beach now and had stopped again to look out at the water. Maybe, she thought, it would have been nice to talk to him.

Katie followed a small gravel road up the valley through two gates, over a ford and then into some trees where a sign said 'Welcome to Happy Valley Community'. From the entrance she could see two buildings, a house and something bigger – a hall, perhaps? In her mind she had pictured five or six simple-looking huts surrounding an overgrown field, but these were proper houses. And there were heaps more of them too, on little side roads that ran off in different directions into the trees as she drove forward. It was as if someone had taken a small suburb out of the city, flown it up the coast and put it down here in the bush. A hundred metres on there was a large garden beside the road. A dozen, maybe twenty, people wearing sunhats stopped work and waved at Katie as she passed. A little embarrassed, she waved back.

The office was a little older than the other houses and closer to the road, but still nothing like the more feral buildings she had expected to find here. She walked up onto the verandah, then paused for a moment staring into the door, wondering what future lay behind it. She liked the way the world was always changing around you, the way your life gave the world history. Today this was just a verandah and a door. Tomorrow it might be the place she met someone or did or realised something important that she would never forget. She took a slow deep breath and knocked. There was a 'Hold on', then a 'Hang on', then finally a 'Come in'. She opened the door.

The room was big. There was a computer, filing cabinets, a large desk and a girl sitting on the other side with big eyes and a friendly smile. She came over and shook Katie's hand.

'Mel?'

'Yes. You must be Katie, come in, sit down ... So, you're from Sydney?'

'Kind of. I grew up there, but I've been down at teachers' college in Melbourne the last few years.'

'I grew up in Sydney too,' Mel said.

'Really? Wow, it must be strange for you to go back there after living in this place,' Katie replied. 'It puts my head in a spin even after Melbourne. For you it must be crazy?'

'I suppose. I left when I was seventeen and I've really only been back once.'

'Why's that?'

'Why have I only been back once?' Mel asked. 'Now there's a question.'

'Cool.'

'What's cool?' Mel asked with a smile.

'Well, I'm just glad you think it's a question,' Katie answered. 'Whenever I ask anyone who doesn't live there about the big city they always say the same stuff: there's not enough space, people are shallow, self-centred, and it's all just so ...'

'Boring?'

'Yes, and bullshit too. People in the city aren't so bad. They're just different from the people who live in the country. But who cares? That's a good thing.'

'Yes, I agree,' replied Mel. 'But I don't think people actually hate people who live in the big city. They just seem easier to blame for things like waste and the homeless and houses that no one can really afford to live in. And none of that is all anyone's fault.'

'You're right, you're right,' said Katie. 'So is it different here? Is it better?'

Mel seemed to consider this for a moment. 'We like it,' she smiled.

'We?' Katie wasn't sure if Mel had meant everyone on the community or someone more specific.

'Yes. I live here with my partner ...' There was a pause. 'You're a very curious person, aren't you?' Mel continued, sitting further back in her chair and looking at Katie with a smile. Katie felt herself blushing. 'No, it's okay,' Mel continued. 'Don't be embarrassed. That's a good thing.'

'Really, you think so?'

'Yeah of course, honest people get answers. It's a gift. It means you won't get wrapped up in all that ego and self-obsession. You'll be above all that crap, you're lucky.'

Katie sighed. 'Sure doesn't feel like that right now.'

Mel smiled back at her again. 'Bit of a rough patch, huh? Oh well, you should have seen me at your age, I was a real mess.'

'But you're not much older than me, are you?' Katie asked.

'Well, that depends. I turn thirty-seven this year?'

'Thirty-seven? Wow. You don't look it.'

'Thanks.'

Katie felt comfortable with Mel. She was the nicest person she'd met in a long time, but when Mel looked up at the clock on the wall behind Katie she seemed to jump a little. 'Hey Katie, I'd like to talk with you some more, but we've got quite a bit to get through yet and I've got other stuff to do so I'd better show you where to go and where things ...'

'Sorry, I didn't mean to keep you.' Katie felt embarrassed again.

'No worries.' Mel sat up and picked a map up off the table. 'And I can't show you around myself, but I can show you where the basics are at least. Then maybe you can just have a wander around by yourself. It's probably a nicer way to see the place anyway.'

Katie nodded. 'Yeah, sure, great.'

Mel pointed to a house in the middle of the map. 'This is the woofers' hut. It's all right, a bit small maybe, but comfortable and it has everything you need. It's right beside the river too, which means ...'

'Mel, I'm sorry,' Katie interrupted a little nervously. 'I'm sure it's nice and everything, but would you mind if I slept in my car? It's a station wagon and well, to be honest, I kind of like to have my own space.'

'Yeah, sure, no worries. There's a carport right beside the woofers' hut, you can park there. And if you've got a net you can sleep with the back door open. It's really nice doing that this time of year. Now this is the community hall where you'll be cooking.' She was pointing to the big building Katie had first seen from the entrance. 'The kitchen's off to the side here. Now we usually eat lunch around twelve thirty, which means that you'll need to start about ten. Pop in there, though, this afternoon if you can. Pat will have started dinner and she can show you where everything is. Now don't mind her too much, Katie. She's a bit funny about who comes into her kitchen but she gets used to you pretty fast if she likes your scent.'

'Will we be cooking together?' Katie asked.

'No, she only cooks the evening meal unless we haven't got a woofer, and we usually do.'

Katie was relieved. It would be nice working by herself.

'Right, now down there's the recreation hall. There's a sauna and a spa behind it which you're most welcome to use. Inside there's dozens of games, couches, a library and heaps of space to just chill out.'

'Wow, there's a library!'

'Yes, you like reading?'

'Yeah, I read all the time. It's one of my favourite things in the world. Have you got many books?'

'Heaps. I started it myself when I first got here. I went around all the second-hand shops and garage sales in the weekends buying up all the books I could. I got trailerloads full and people have been adding to it ever since so it's just got bigger and bigger.'

Katie glanced down at the map. 'And how many people live here?'

'There are thirty-two permanents and now, including you, five woofers. But over Christmas or the school holidays there can be hundreds.'

'Hundreds?'

'Most of the children go to boarding school and they just love bringing their friends home here for the holidays, so it can get pretty mad, but it gives the place a good airing out too, if you know what I mean.' Mel paused, then handed Katie the little map. 'So that's about it then,' she said, standing up. 'And I guess I'll catch up with you a bit more at dinner.'

The carport seemed overgrown, but just driving in the car pushed down most of the weeds and when she had found the flattest spot she stopped, opened up the back door and took out the carpet and put it over the rest of the weeds below her feet. She then rearranged things inside a little again to make room for her mattress, which she rolled out from one end to the other. She then arranged her incense holder, her wallet, her keys, her cellphone, a book, her handbag, her lighter and her tobacco on either side and when she'd finished she rolled a cigarette and sat with her back against the front seat. She could see parts of the river twenty or thirty metres down the bank. She lit the cigarette, exhaled and smiled.

There was no one in the woofers' house when she went inside a while later. She could hear running water, so someone may have been in the shower, but it didn't seem worth hanging around to find out, not when she had a whole new world to explore. Further up the road lots of people were still out working in the garden. The way they stopped and watched her made Katie feel a little uncomfortable at first, yet there was something really honest and friendly about it that she appreciated. People in the city always looked away when you caught them watching you, and these people were nice, polite. They simply waited until she smiled and then smiled back.

A little further on the road passed beside the river so she climbed down a small bank to put her feet in the water. It was cool between her toes. When she carried on up the road, she turned onto the track to the sauna. It wasn't like the ones you would find in a hotel. Down the end of a bush path, made out of half-logs and tin bound together with some rusty-looking wire, it had lots of charm. Sitting in there when it was cold outside, listening to the crisp sound of the running water nearby, would be fantastic.

The recreation hall was the most impressive building yet. Like the sauna, it was built in a more offbeat fashion than the houses, with lots of naked timber and tin. It was made up of two levels separated by a wooden ladder. On the bottom level stood a pool table and a couple of couches and upstairs a dozen or so low beds under an A-frame roof that was flanked at either end by walls made almost entirely of glass, making you feel as if you were standing in the bush. It was really beautiful, and Kate could just imagine all the community's kids running around in there at night. They'd think it was heaven.

The library was in the same building behind a dark brown door at the back of the downstairs room. It was so dark and creepy-looking that at first Katie was almost frightened to go over and open it, but she was glad she did. All her favourites were there, from William Blake to Anne Rice, Bill Bryson to J.K. Rowling, Aldous Huxley to up-and-coming Canadian writer Nina Gilbert. She sat reading for a while before heading for the kitchen.

Pat, the cook, was a middle-aged Irish woman who looked a little less pleased with the world than most people would like to be. She had a temper, too – Katie could feel that even though their conversation was mild. She took time away from her dinner preparations to show Katie around the kitchen, only mentioning the inconvenience ten or twelve times. She showed her where the cutlery and cups were, the plates and pots, detailing all the food in the pantry, explaining when it was stocked up and what to do if something ran out. There were a few peculiarities, like the coal range and the big ice-box that doubled as a fridge when they had to keep food for longer than a day, but 'most of it's fresh from the garden or the farm,' she explained.

'We get rats too,' Pat continued. 'You got to watch out for the rats.'

'Rats!' Katie exclaimed, sensing this was a topic Pat might want to elaborate on, and amused that it could be.

'Well, one rat. The general we call him. I've only ever seen him once, and big, oh yeah he's real big, the general. We put traps down of course, but he's way too smart for them, the general, way too smart.' Pat's body and voice had slowed as she told Katie about the rat, and she seemed to be staring off into the distance. She was different too, happier somehow, and it made Katie smile.

'You don't have to dish it out,' Pat continued. 'Just put the food up there on the serving benches and the plates and cutlery on the bench and people will help themselves. They do their own dishes mostly, but you'll need to hang around afterwards just to make sure. We don't want the general getting too fat while I'm not here.'

The other woofers were in the house when Katie got back. Sam was a young English guy in his mid-twenties who wanted to start an organic garlic farm when he got back home. He had learnt a lot, he told Katie, who smiled and tried not to lose interest when two minutes describing how to grow onions and garlic organically turned into twenty. Blair and Steve, two gay guys from Canada, were friendly but so much in love that they sat gazing into each other's eyes most of the time without ever taking more than a polite interest in the world and people around them. Katie didn't like them so much, but she did like Jean, a young Aussie girl who explained she had ended up here between hitchhiking rides about a year ago.

Katie sat out in her car a while before dinner, smoking a cigarette and reflecting on the day. Things were going well so far. She had a nice private place to relax, a library to visit, work was going to be fun and she had made a new friend. She stubbed out the cigarette and was just about to leave when she remembered the man from the beach. She could see him clearly in her mind now, only he was no longer looking out to sea; he had turned around and was looking at her.

Dinner was less formal than she expected. The people talked, but their conversations weren't organised or serious. They simply came in, ate their meal, lost and found their kids a few times, then left. A few talked to her, but she was too distracted to concentrate properly. She couldn't stop thinking about the man at the beach. Who was he? Would she see him again? 'Are you all right?' Mel asked, sitting down beside her after most people had eaten and the room had started to clear. 'I'm sorry I had to chase you out so quickly this afternoon.'

Katie shook her head. 'It's okay. And I'm okay, I think, just a bit tired. I'll be fine after a good night's sleep.'

It was a full moon that night and lying in her bed looking out the back door of the car Katie found herself remembering the time her dad had got a migraine while driving up to Brisbane and they'd checked into a motel in Byron Bay for the night. She was maybe fourteen or fifteen and she had gone out for a walk. It was just on dusk, the sun slipping behind the hills somewhere behind the town where a man had paid a sand sculptor to write 'Kylie, I love you. Will you marry me?' on the side of a huge sand castle he had built that day on the beach. Kylie had almost screamed when she saw it, and then after the laughing subsided and much to the relief of the watching crowd, and of her boyfriend, she said yes. The two then kissed and everyone cheered. Katie had cried. It was the most romantic thing she had ever seen. She knew why she had remembered it now. She could see the man's face in her mind, almost floating above the ocean in front of her as she drifted off to sleep smiling.

Katie arrived in the kitchen just before ten. Pat had left all the instructions she needed on the bench beside the sink. She was to prepare pumpkin soup, home-made bread, the usual tea and coffee, raspberry cordial and scones for after. First off she lit the coal range and tended the fire until it was well established. Then she lifted the three large pumpkins up onto the bench and hacked them in half with the largest knife she could find, and then into smaller pieces and put them all in the biggest pot with cold water and set it down on the coal range. The bread was easier to make than she'd thought. Once she'd looked at the instructions and realised that it was just a scone mixture of butter and flour and baking powder prepared and cooked in a slightly different way, she carried on without too much drama, even saving herself some work by preparing the scones and the bread together before baking them separately. She then started sliding them into the coal range on trays, two or three at a time, setting them down on a rack above to keep them warm when they came out. Later she added milk, butter, pepper, salt and spices to the pumpkin soup and let it thicken. She liked cooking on the coal range: it made her feel like a colonial woman cooking a meal for the hungry men carving out their own new world in the wilderness.

Katie took a deep breath. With the fresh breeze coming in though the windows, the aroma of freshly cooked food pleasing her senses and the satisfaction of having achieved something good, she felt more satisfied than she had in a long time. Could this be the thing that she was meant to do? She had enjoyed it more than any day at teachers' college or any moment of those horrible placements where she had really begun to see that, even though she liked kids, she sure as hell didn't want to spend the rest of her life around them. It wouldn't pay much but she'd rather live somewhere like this and eat and live well and not have to worry than be somewhere else slaving her guts out just to get by. In the quiet she could hear the birds singing again. She listened for a moment then got back to work, pulling the last of the baking out of the oven, mixing the cordial and assembling the plates and spoons and knives on the bench. Then she stood proudly, ready to help when the first person walked through the door. She had done well.

Over lunch people talked much more than they had at dinner the night before. They all seemed excited by the day's activities. Five or six of them were building a new house up the road out of mud brick. Other people had been gardening or baking or painting or making things out of wood and fabric. One man was an artist, another a writer, another made drums. There were pre-school children there too, who played and ate happily at their own little table in the corner. It was like a party.

As Katie started back down the hill to the woofers' hut, she saw something move into the bush just in front of her. It had happened so fast that it took a moment to comprehend that it was a person. And, more than that, it was the man she'd seen at the beach. She walked quickly to where he'd disappeared, then stopped. He was already out of sight.

She decided to follow. The bush quickly grew darker and thicker and she was soon moving more and more slowly. Five minutes passed, then ten. She kept stopping to see if she could hear his footsteps in front of her, but there was nothing. She kept on. She was a fair way from the community now: if she screamed no one would hear her. She was beginning to feel a bit scared, yet she had to keep going.

There was light ahead, a space, the bush was opening up again.

She crept right up to the edge of the small clearing and took a deep breath. What an extraordinary place. It was a flat patch of ground at the bottom of a tiny valley, with thick bush running up the hills around it in every direction. There were chickens, a pig that slept lazily in the afternoon sun, a goat, a couple of sheep – and it was so quiet, so peaceful. There was a house too, but it wasn't a normal house. It didn't even have four walls, but a series of half-walls supplemented by curtains and large windows and verandahs that opened up in every direction. There was no front or back and the whole thing – not just the bed or a single room but the whole house – was inside a gigantic white muslin mosquito net. It was so beautiful, so perfect and so secret. The word brought back the fear. She looked around. Where was he? Her pulse began to pick up again. Suddenly the house began to seem more strange than beautiful, more dangerous than exotic. She took another step backwards, then stopped. There was a noise behind her. A branch breaking. He was there. She turned around.

Her fear left her straight away. He was even more beautiful and gentle and shy than he had been in her mind. He still had the wild hair and there was a flicker of something wild in his eyes too, but it wasn't the type of wildness that would ever hurt anyone. The confusion she had seen at the beach was gone now too and his face was peaceful. A few seconds passed. They stood watching each other.

'You were at the beach yesterday. You watched me.'

'You saw me?' she asked, a little confused.

'No,' he replied, 'but I had a feeling someone was there.' He smiled a little.

'How did you know I would follow you up here?' she asked, smiling a little too.

'I didn't.' He looked away from her shyly. 'I just hoped you would. I wanted to talk to you. I saw you at dinner last night and sitting out on the verandah just now.'

'And is this where you live?' she asked.

'Yes.'

'It's an amazing place. So private. You could do anything you like here.' She felt herself blushing and avoiding his brown eyes. He was even more attractive than she had imagined.

'Would you like me to show you around?' he asked.

Katie took a moment to answer. All of a sudden she felt a little nervous herself. He liked her too. Oh my God, he liked her too.

As she followed him around the yard he told her about his plants, his animals and living almost self-sufficiently, then he led her under the mosquito net and into the house.

Inside it was a little untidy, with bare timber and art materials and coins and bottles everywhere, but it was also very cosy and Katie felt very comfortable. In the kitchen he told her how he sometimes made pasta from scratch, using eggs that his chickens laid and wheat that he grew, then ground into flour.

'How long have you lived here?' she asked.

'A couple of years, maybe ten,' he answered with a little laugh.

She looked at the guitar beside the sink. She could imagine him playing it on the porch in a cool summer breeze, the music settling like dust all around this secret little valley, soothing the animals and the bush where it brushed over rocks and whistled through the trees. She closed her eyes for a second and imagined what it would be like to live here. What it would be like to be naked and bathe in the rain outside. What it would be like to wake up here in the morning and know that you had the whole day to be here, free of everything, safe from everything.

Katie sat down on the corner of the bed and watched him make tea. 'You have a really beautiful house,' she said.

'Thank you,' he replied simply.

When he was sitting beside her with the tea she said, 'Hi, my name's Katie. How do you do?' They both laughed.

'Hey Katie. My name's Sean.'

He asked her about the city and her degree and she asked him about the community and his life. He told her he liked it there because no one ever pressured him into doing anything he didn't want to do. He didn't even have to go and eat dinner if he didn't want to, and he didn't need money because when he sold his house in Sydney ten years ago it had given him enough money to buy this piece of land, build this house and buy food and clothes for the rest of his life. He was ten years older than her, but that didn't matter. No boy near her age had made her feel as comfortable, relaxed and happy.

'Are you hungry?' he asked after they had shared three cigarettes, a joint he rolled from a tin and two more cups of tea.

'Yes.' She moved herself around to lie on the bed facing the kitchen. 'Starving.'

'Well then, let's cook,' he said standing up and wobbling a bit.

After they had eaten they sat and talked for a few more hours. It was nice, really nice, and the touching and the sex was nice too, and the laughter, and the waking up the next morning with the trees and the birds, and the smell of freshly brewed coffee wafting right through this magical little valley, where she was no longer a lonely alien girl powerless in a strange world but a queen in her own kingdom, with her own beautiful and loving king.

At half past ten she raced back down the path toward the community. She could feel herself smiling, and she even laughed out loud a few times. Back at the car beside the woofers' hut she quickly changed her clothes – no time for a shower this morning.

She got back to the kitchen just before eleven and found the instructions and ingredients Pat had left her. Stir-fried tofu and vegetables and rice. Good. That would be easy and quick enough. She couldn't wait to tell Mel all about what had happened. Sean was perfect – earthy, peaceful, fun. And she felt so good around him, so at home. Maybe he would ask her to live there with him.

She'd only had two boyfriends before and they were nice guys, but they were young and it had been too much about quick, awkward sex and not enough about reality and feelings and, did she dare think it, love.

Katie was hungry but also eager to see and talk with Mel, so she stood waiting beside the kitchen for her to come in. But when most of the people had eaten and there was still no sign of Mel, she ate quickly, put some of the stir-fried vegetables and rice on a plate and then wrapped it all up in a plastic bag.

The front door to Mel's office was closed and as Katie walked up the stairs to the verandah she suddenly had a strange and unpleasant feeling that maybe something was wrong. She walked across to the door and stopped and listened. She couldn't hear anything. She knocked quietly. There was a silence for a moment and then Katie could hear someone fumbling around inside.

'Mel? It's me, Katie. I've brought you some lunch.'

There was another silence then Katie could hear footsteps up to the door.

'Mel, are you okay?' She asked.

There was another short pause, then the door handle turned and the door opened a little and Mel looked at her through the gap.

'Mel, what's wrong?' Mel had been crying and seemed a little embarrassed. She let go of the door and it swung open a little more and she started crying openly again. Katie put the plate down, stepped forward and put her arms around her.

'It's okay,' she said. 'It'll be all right.'

After a while she talked Mel into sitting down on the verandah and eating her lunch, and then she started to seem a little better.

'Thank you for lunch,' Mel said. 'It was really nice. You're a good cook, Katie, you know that?'

'Well, to be honest, I was kind of rushed this morning.' Katie almost smiled, remembering why she was in a hurry, but caught herself just in time.

Mel let out a little laugh.

'What's funny?' Katie asked.

'My life,' Mel said. 'And men.'

'Is that what you're upset about? Your partner?'

Mel looked at her a moment and nodded ever so slightly.

'Why, what happened?' Katie asked.

Mel looked up at her more seriously. 'I think he's been cheating.'

'How do you know?'

'I don't, that's just what's driving me mad.'

'Have you confronted him?'

Mel glanced at her again. 'No. Do you think I should?'

'Why not?'

'I don't know,' she said. 'I guess maybe I'm too scared of the answer.'

The walk up the bush path seemed a lot shorter than it had yesterday, and it was certainly less intense. Katie was still a little upset about what had happened with Mel. Poor girl. Maybe she could tell Sean about it; he might know the man she'd been involved with. She was interested to know what sort of guy Mel would be interested in. She was a lot like her in some ways – the same build, similar hair and social manner. Maybe her taste in guys was similar, too.

She came to a halt at the edge of the clearing. It was quiet again, really quiet. Maybe he'd heard her coming up the path and had hidden again to surprise her. She looked behind her, but he wasn't there. She called, 'Sean, Sean …' but there was no reply. She started over toward the house. Suddenly she had a bad feeling again. She lifted up the mosquito net and walked up onto the verandah and into the house. It was just as she had left it this morning. The bed was not made and the dishes from their meal the night before were still in the sink. He had to be here somewhere. She was just about to call out again when something caught her eye. There was a note on the bench: '*Katie, make yourself at home. Back soon. XXXX Sean.*'

She let out a deep sigh and lay down on the bed with the note in her hand. Maybe now she could even have a snooze while she waited. She closed her eyes and was just drifting off when she heard something in the distance – footsteps on gravel. Someone was coming up the path. She would surprise him. She looked around for somewhere to hide. There was a cupboard with a laundry basket on top so she squeezed herself in and left the door open just enough to see him come in. She waited, the footsteps got louder, came into the clearing, but it wasn't Sean. It was Mel.

Mel stopped by the house. '*Sean!*' she yelled. There was no reply. Oh shit. Was she going to come in the house? Katie didn't want Mel to see her here. *Please don't come in here,* she whispered under her breath. *Please, please don't come in here.* Mel looked around. '*Sean!*' she called out again. 'Sean, are you here?' When there was no reply she left.

An hour later Katie sat in the front seat of her car. How could it be like this? How could life be so cruel? She tried to roll a cigarette but started to cry before she could finish it. Why did things have to go sour when they were so perfect? It was such a cool place, she could have stayed and been happy and at home for a long time. Sean and Mel were both so friendly, so nice. In a way she almost wanted to go over and apologise to Mel, but what could she say? Thanks for having me, I really enjoyed the food and the nature and the night with your boyfriend. No, it was time to leave. What a wanker Sean was. He'd watched her, then waited for her. It hadn't just happened, that was for sure. And how many times had he done that before? He seemed so genuine. Maybe she should tell Mel – serve him right, the bastard. She started the car, pulled out of the carport and slowed down in front of Mel's office. Should she stop? Yes. She couldn't just leave like this.

Her heart was beating fast now. She knocked. 'Just a moment,'

Mel said. 'Coming.' She sounded happier now. As the door opened, Katie stepped back. Mel looked at her, then at the packed car, then back at her.

'Katie, what's wrong? Why are you leaving?'

Katie was really nervous now. She should have kept going.

Mel stepped forward and touched her arm. 'Katie, are you all right?'

Katie took a big breath. 'I think I slept with your boyfriend.'

'But how? When?'

'Last night,' Katie answered.

'But ...'

'I'm really sorry, I didn't mean it. It was just that he was so nice, and charming. I saw him at the beach on the way out here and then he came out of the bush yesterday and I followed him up the path to his house and we just hit it off. I had no idea he was your boyfriend, Mel. Really, I had no idea. He never said he had a girlfriend either and if I'd known he did I'd never have done it, especially if I'd known it was you.'

'But Katie ...' Mel said again quietly.

'I'd never,' she continued, 'have even dreamed of doing anything like that ...'

'Katie,' Mel said, this time a little louder, and Katie stopped. The look on Mel's face was no longer angry or even shocked. 'Matt was with me last night.'

'Matt?' Katie was confused. 'But he said his name was Sean.'

'It is, if it's who I think you're talking about, and he's not my boyfriend. My boyfriend's name is Matt and he was with me last night.'

'But I saw you ...' Katie stopped herself saying it. She didn't want Mel to know she'd been hiding.

'You saw me where?'

Katie thought for a moment. 'I saw you go up there to confront him this afternoon after we talked.'

'Katie, I know Sean. He's a friend of mine and I went up there to see him this afternoon to ask him for some advice, but he wasn't home.'

'So that means I didn't ...' Katie began.

'No,' Mel answered. She stepped forward and touched Katie's arm again. 'And so I guess you might be staying around for a while then.'

RaNDoM

ARE YOU A man or a woman, gay or straight, young or old? Do your feet touch the ground or dangle from intellectual heights? Do you know yourself, or have other people told you what and who you are? Are you nothing or everything?

Do you want to enjoy what you have or be angry about what you don't? Do you like what you see or loathe the view? Do you long to see the sun or crave the rain?

Are you driven to success? Are you enjoying the drive? Would you race to your next meeting with your strung-up, strung-out, always wanting more partner, or stroll some forgotten field of flowers with someone you love?

Do you want to live quickly? Are you racing against time? Do you think you'll beat it, or are you taking a few moments to decide?

Do you want to die? Do you think about it a lot? The ways it could happen. How you might react. Or are you scared of living, and of what life might do to you? Are you caught up in the pain? Do you think you'll last?

Are you pleased with who you are? Where you're going and the choices you've made? Or does it all seem like someone else's words now? Something you just say?

Do you blame yourself or tell others they're the problem?

Do you crave? Feel love bursting between your legs? Does it run down your legs, your arms? Do your fingers long to touch? To caress yourself and others? Do you want it? Do you really?

Do you dress to impress or live in neglect? Do you seldom treat yourself or do you fill yourself up with crap all the time? Do you celebrate when you feel like other people might feel like you are normal, or do you rejoice in your difference?

Are you an individual? Do you feel alone? Does your mind give off a low hum that only you can hear, that no one else could possibly understand? Does it soak you with unwanted thoughts, choke up your airways? Trap you? Scare you into submission? Do you want to be someone else? To say all the right things? To never get it wrong? To have a flawless past, a bright future, to always be part of the in-crowd?

Do you want to win at all costs? Will you share the success or keep pushing people away?

Do you live in fear? Do you want it to end? To stay in bed and never get up? Will your mind turn cold, freeze up and stop? Are you scared of who you are, or that you're not what your parents think, or your friends? Are you afraid of what you've said or even what you've thought? Is it your world or are you a stranger in your own life?

Do you long for change, for daydreams, for love, for hate, for beauty, for fame, for fortune, for comfort, for ease, for the sky, for enlightenment, acceptance? Will you dive into the depths of passion? Will it radiate from you like fire? Or do you desire simple perfection? Justification, acceptance, correctness?

Do you want to plant your seed wherever and whenever you can, or do you really just want to be held? Appreciated? Do you always want to be in love? Would you stay in the warm for just a little love, or go out in the cold to find a lot?

Are you asking the right questions or answering to someone else's bullshit? Are you being honest about it all? Are you really?

Caught Out

It's always interesting hitching in winter. Those who've done it will know what I mean. It's different in summer. Time's on your side, and if you're not home by eight there's no great need to panic, because it's still light and someone might still pick you up. And failing that, you know that you can always just sleep under a tree or in a school without any great risk to your health.

In the winter it pays to get going early, and if you happen to be one of those people who doesn't get out of bed until after noon it pays to get the bus. On this particular day, right in the middle of winter, I had to hitch home. It was four days into the holiday and I'd been putting it off too long. Unfortunately, and contrary to the best of my intentions, I slept all morning and didn't rise from my cot until after most good working folk had finished their lunch break. I wasn't up the hill at hitchers' post until well after two.

For the first half an hour or so I was still half asleep, my eyes scanning the dark clouds smothering the sky above me. Rain was something I could do without. Around three o'clock I was beginning to get worried. Even though home was only two hours away, and if I got a ride now I could easily make it before it got dark, there were bugger-all cars on the road, and even fewer were taking any interest in me, or my need to get home for a decent meal. When another half-hour rolled around I was looking at my watch every thirty seconds or so, thinking more and more that I might have to spend another night at the flat. This would be all right normally, but I was the last to leave and there was no food left, and I had no money to buy anything. I decided to give it until four thirty, and if I wasn't travelling north by then I'd walk back down the hill. I'd been in worse predicaments. I wouldn't die of hunger, and there was always the TV to keep me company.

Having come to this decision I managed to relax a little, quit looking at my watch and settled into a rather less intense and more reflective train of thought. Many things had happened that semester and it was nice to let the activities, the pranks, the voices come into my mind.

Pete hitched a lot, sometimes, he claimed, just for fun. He told me a lot of stories about his adventures too – he was very proud of them – but one tale suddenly seemed brighter and more colourful that the rest. You see, Pete was the biggest bullshit artist I'd ever met in my life, and he had one of the most active imaginations. He was entertaining too, and I guess that's why people put up with him. I think we knew, though, when he was lying, even if we never said. And I guess, now that I think about it, hopping in and out of strangers' cars would have been great for Pete. Each would have been a new opportunity, a new page on which to paint his pictures, perfect his craft. For one ride he could be a PhD student of astrophysics; the next he might have as easily been spouting off some great spiel about saving the rainforest with a new serum he was working on. The truth, of course, was that Pete was a first-year arts student who was thus far failing miserably.

Anyway, that day a particular notion came over me. Why couldn't I do the same? It might be fun. Yeah, why not? If I got a ride, bugger it, I'd do it. My imagination was nothing compared with Pete's, but the worst thing that could happen was that I could slip up and the driver would know that I was talking shit. Still, he could only get offended, only kick me out in the middle of nowhere, and would I really be any worse off?

The horn made me jump. A red Mazda had pulled in. I had a ride.

'How far you going?'

'Timaru,' I replied to the driver, whose wife looked at me from the passenger seat.

'We're going right through to Christchurch. Hop in.'

I was as good as home. I climbed into the back seat.

The first couple of glances I stole at the man in the rear-vision mirror left me with the impression that I'd seen him before. However, I could only see an inch above and below his eyes so I wasn't sure and after a while I simply dismissed the idea. It was a long ride, too, so the conversation was slow to start, and beginning to relax, I sat back and once again returned to reflecting on the semester, forgetting all about my plan to reinvent myself. So when the question did come, after a few kilometres, it took me by surprise.

'So,' the man said, 'are you studying?'

I froze. I hadn't determined exactly what I was going to say. Panic raced through my mind. I stuttered. What would he be thinking? That I couldn't answer his simple question? I considered telling the truth, but I was too panicky, and even the truth seemed vague in my mind. And then, to my surprise, the answer just fell from my lips. 'I'm doing my PhD,' I said.

'Well, that sounds very interesting,' the man replied, seemingly untroubled by my hesitation. But in the pause that followed, my mind was anything but silent. It raced uncontrollably. More questions were now inevitable and I had to have answers ready. Good, believable answers.

'So what's your thesis about?'

I considered the truth, an early confession, something to let me off the hook, but the answer again just dropped from my lips. 'My thesis is quite complex, and not easy to explain, but it's basically about the supernatural. But it doesn't really deal with the supernatural in any exterior way. Rather it aims to discuss and, I hope, to come to some conclusion as to the need for the supernatural inside an individual, if that makes any sense.'

It was lies, of course, but I saw the man raise an eyebrow and, hell, I think I even raised one of my own.

It's amazing how much you can talk about something when you put your mind to it, even when you're just making it up. For the following hour I completely laid out my fictional project to the man and his wife. I told them all the ins and outs, I told them about my human subjects, to whom I even managed to give names and lives that sounded quite realistic. I wouldn't have continued for so long, but they just seemed so fascinated by it all. I'd never talked so much shit in my life. It felt great. And I don't think I slipped up once. And when I did finally stop talking, I felt myself beaming. It was marvellous. It was as if my ego had been given some massive shot of adrenaline. No wonder, I thought, as we neared Timaru, Pete was so happy all the time.

When we got into town the driver asked me if I lived far off the main drag.

'Yes,' I replied, feeling awfully full of myself. And feeling as if I'd done him a favour, I accepted his offer of a ride right to my door.

We pulled up outside my parents' house about six and the man came around the car to shake my hand. I thanked him for the ride without really looking him in the face. When he was back on the driver's side he stopped before he got back in and looked at me. It was the first time I had seen his whole face.

'If you can spin a yarn like that, mate, I look forward to your essays next semester.'

He left me standing there, mouth open, as he turned the car around. I could see his wife smiling. He'd been introduced to us in last Friday's philosophy lecture, when I was dozing at the front of the class. He would be our lecturer in the second semester.

Diamonds Don't Shine in the Dark

FLOWERS ARE THE most precious thing in the world to me. They shine in the sunlight like God's little diamonds and I love everything about them. But these days, between work and meetings and classes and all the gay social functions we attend, I only really get to see them at night. After we've got home, finished our dinner, walked the dog and poured second drinks, we go out and enjoy the garden. We do this every evening. It's our own private little ritual. Alex knows how much it means to me, of course; he always makes an effort to be there and he never complains that the gardener costs too much. So you can see why it hit us both so hard, why we reacted with such passion when the flowers in our special little garden started to go missing.

At first it didn't matter so much. He was only taking the ones at the back and neither Alex nor I could see them anyway. But then he started stealing the ones at the front, tainting our moonlit evenings with a bitterness that grew and grew until finally we couldn't enjoy any of the flowers at all. How could he do such a thing? How could he possess such a twisted Lack of Respect, such a bitter Contempt for People's Rights, for their possessions, for their flowers – their flowers, for God's sake!

We'd figured out who he was, of course. There was no mystery in that. He was the man who sold flowers in Newtown on Saturday and Sunday afternoons. I'd even bought his flowers for Alex a couple of times. Little did either of us know then that what I was paying for probably already belonged to us. So, after a near sleepless night and a lot of discussion, we decided we would approach him on the following Saturday afternoon. Give him a Jolly Good Piece of Our Mind. Alex was especially excited; he had seen what this Evil Criminal had done to me, and he was going to make him pay. Although, to be honest, I wasn't even sure any more if that was the real reason at all. I was mad, yet we had to be careful, approach it correctly. Alex and I are accepted here in Newtown; we have friends, a Reputation, and it wouldn't do to make a scene. But I didn't have to worry – it didn't even happen. After lunch we marched up Church Street, past the dog park, on to King, where we found him in his usual spot, taking gold coins from smiling faces outside the IGA supermarket. But I couldn't do it, I changed my mind before we got to him. Alex urged me to go on of course, to see it through. 'That bastard stole our flowers, Craig!' he yelled. 'Our flowers!' I turned around and told him that I was going home. When he insisted and raised his voice, I promised him that I would explain if he followed me back to the dog park which, after a little more protest and a look of bewilderment, then frustration, he agreed to do.

I didn't really know what I was going to say to Alex when we got back to the park. I only knew that something changed in me when we got close to the young man selling our flowers. I saw something in his eyes that I hadn't seen in anyone else's for a long time. I'm not sure if it was desperation or desire, whether it was good or bad or anything else, only that it was different. Different from me, different from my world. All of a sudden it didn't seem to matter whether we had fifty-eight flowers in our garden or fifty-six. Why should I care really? Things are good for us, and who knows what life is like for other people? Who knows what goes on behind their eyes and behind the walls we all help to build? Not me. Not me. I don't want to play God, dishing out punishment to people I don't know, living lives I don't understand.

And you know what, after that those flowers seemed more precious and valuable and beautiful to me than ever. And if they were destined to shine in someone else's life, then that was okay too.

SuCCess

REMEMBER THE FIRST time I saw those black and white plastic bags. It was in my last year of school. I was sitting with a small group of my friends outside a café on the main street. We had all skipped fifth period and the shit school canteen food for somewhere a little more 'grown up' and I had zoned out of the conversation when Sarah started talking about some new pair of shoes she'd just bought. Head full of boredom and frustration, I looked up and, catching sight of a pretty common main street image, had a less than common main street thought. The man walking with the black and white NRGTH bag was good-looking, proud, unquestionable. He walked happily, enjoying the attention and the moment, knowing that everyone wanted to be like him. Everyone wanted to receive an invitation to shop in that store, to be seen walking with one of those bags. Everyone except me.

I remember trying to arouse my friends' curiosity that day but it was pointless. They were more accepting of their lives and of our reality than I was. And there were Sarah's shoes to think about. I did, however, manage to get them to wait while I tried to enter the NRGTH shop on the way back to sixth period. They only wanted me to read the sign, telling me that it was stupid to try and go in. They were right, too: I was met halfway up the stairs by a large man dressed in a black jacket who asked me to leave and not come back again without an invitation. But how they weren't completely taken with this new mystery I couldn't work out. Why this icon, this symbol of success, of class separation, presented so plainly in front of us, wasn't as fascinating and as tempting to them was a mystery to me. Maybe it was because back then their lives made a little more sense than my own. They'd been approved, they had certainty. They knew what they wanted to do and were comfortable with how they fitted into things, where they shopped, what they could afford. They knew where they were going, whereas I was always far less sure, more up in the air, liable to be swept away, taken in, left out. But things change quickly in your youth: a younger person's day is fast, with moods that change so often; adults are slower and more used to time. So I left the mystery on the main street that day and returned to school and to my life and didn't think seriously about it again for nearly five years.

I would love to have some good things to say about those five years, those years of 'freedom' between leaving high school and finding my financial feet. There's the odd flicker of memory that isn't so bad, but it was pretty ordinary, really. Even if individuals could truly be liberated in this society (and of course they can't), there's still the question of survival. And society makes it harder and harder the less you have, and it's difficult to believe that 'less is more' when you don't have any food, when you're hungry and crawling along the bottom, finding it impossible to climb back up. It may have been okay to live like that once, but it's just not practical any more. Society wants you to want everything. It needs you to be greedy. It's how life works. And, regrettably, how it worked for me. So I wandered and wondered and had my time of 'freedom'.

I was in almost exactly the same spot when it happened. I'd only been passing through town, staying at my parents' house for a few nights that had become a few weeks because I was having trouble scraping the money together to move on. And so, down on my luck and having slept too late again to do much else, I decided to head up to the main street and spend my last three bucks on a coffee. I used to do that a lot back then – spending my last money on a luxury item rather than an essential one. It worked sometimes too, pretending to be rich when I was really poor, and some good stuff did come out of it. I used to think back then that poverty was a state of mind, that you were either above or below it, and that the decision was made in your own head rather than by what was in your pocket ... So, anyway, I was sitting there enjoying my coffee, thinking about nothing in particular, when, all of sudden, those bags came walking back into my life.

Brandon James, a boy from my old school, was carrying one. He was only a couple of years older than me. A football head. An arrogant, good-looking prick who was, I suppose, charming enough inside his own circle back then, but despised by everybody else outside it. And there he was, right there in front of me, with his new girlfriend and the bags. Obviously there were others out there who found his manner charming, or maybe, as he had done in school, he'd just learnt to manipulate the hierarchy. I imagined his life. His job that would be more title than anything else. A marketing degree probably, privileged ownership of just enough restricted information about a system to be able to write a report demonstrating his rule over the people within it. I sat watching the stupid look of satisfaction on his face, imagining him explaining his own success, taking credit, thinking that his life was just as hard, and that he understood, or worse, knew better than everybody else. God, it made me mad seeing him then, so wrongfully admired. I remember my cheeks brightening with rage until my thoughts blazed and my fist started beating down on the table.

That's how it started. The first change. Everyone said they could hardly recognise me afterward, I was so different. My parents said they thought the transition was funny, but I think they laughed more from relief than amusement. They hadn't liked my vagrant existence, you see, and watching me go out for coffee as an aloof twenty-something university dropout, and come back as a success-focused young man, was a dream come true for them. It didn't matter that I was doing it because I had something to prove, or because I wanted something so badly and was suddenly so obsessed by it that I would have killed for it. It only mattered that I had changed, that I was the same as them now, acceptable. For a while anyway.

I was completely possessed by greed, by a hunger and a lust the likes of which I'd neither experienced in myself nor seen in anybody else. I knew what I wanted and I went about getting it – in the day, and in my dreams. Brandon James's pursuits were mild compared with my own. The lies he told were mere fabrications compared with the manipulations I performed. Of course, as my obsession grew, parts of the world did shut their doors to me, as I'm sure they must have always been closed to Brandon. But the financial world made up for their lack of response, and my accumulation was fast and vigorous.

But it wasn't enough. The thing I wanted most of all hadn't arrived yet: the invitation to that store. The right to get those bags and to own whatever was inside them. It was time for a change of tack. To tell the lies and make the friends I needed. To be charming on the outside the way that Brandon James had always been. How hard could it be to be tidy and well presented, to say the right things and know the right people, to change your life and who you were to get the things you thought you wanted? Not that I made any real friends, because after the invitation came and quenched my curiosity, I guess I lost it a bit, went off the rails, and none of them really wanted to know me after that. I had too much money to be put away, and after a while I settled down again when I finally began to understand what had happened, how I ticked, what I needed. Because it's more than just balance, it's truth as well.

And the truth of those black and white bags? They were society's biggest lie of all. Sure, people looked at me when I walked past that day, smiling at me with something between jealousy, admiration and hate. But when I got home, closed and locked the doors and was finally alone to read over the contract I'd signed in the store, which stated that I could never tell another person what was in the bags, I looked inside. There was nothing there.

Taking the Fall

THEY DIDN'T SPEAK as they drove out of the city. There was nothing to say. They were all locked in now, their three separate fates about to become one.

Adrian looked out the window and saw the gas station where he had once stopped with his girlfriend. To lighten the mood, he thought of telling the others about how they had got it on in the toilets, but decided against it.

Michael watched the truck stop come and go where his old man had told him that he wouldn't be going back with him the next day. That he would be going back by himself in the truck to pick up their stuff and that the two of them would be living in a new house in Brisbane from then on. He could still hear his father yelling that his mother was 'a no-good cheating ...' after Michael had asked 'why' so many times that he'd lost his temper and given him an answer. It still covered Michael with that same sickly feeling too. He hated his father for that feeling, and for what he did to his mother when he got back to Sydney.

Peter saw where he had pulled his first stick up at the Mobil station just north of Asquith. He remembered the intensity, the rush, the thrill of the chase, how good the blade had looked against the attendant's throat and how he had tingled all over when it pierced his skin. It hadn't mattered that he'd got caught, or that he went away. He could see where he'd gone wrong, and he would do it again and get it right when he got out. And he did, again and again, until it wasn't enough any more and he needed something else to fill the gap.

If they'd been talking, Adrian may have told them that despite how today might end up he was glad for the opportunity. Things hadn't been so shit-hot since Wendy left and he'd needed to change something. Michael might have talked about the plan, made sure that everyone knew what they were doing, where they needed to be and what to do if things went wrong. Peter liked the silence – it gave him time to think, to consider and enjoy the seriousness of what he was about to do. Inside his stomach, Adrian's nerves swam like fish in a new pond. Michael sat chewing his gum looking out the window and Peter drove, his right hand fidgeting excitedly between the seat and the door where no one could see.

Outside the car the kilometres were passing and soon enough they were taking a left off the main street, another right and a final left onto Rockdale Terrace. They parked outside number thirty-three, just a few houses away from thirty-nine.

'How long till he gets here?'

'Ten minutes.'

'Ten minutes?'

'Maybe twelve.'

'Twelve?'

'Eleven.' The numbers changed on Michael's watch when he looked at it the second time. A sense of urgency exploded in the air. They sat up. They needed to go over the plan. Peter had to deal with the security van's driver, so he'd researched the route and his movements. He'd studied it on the map, come up here last week to look over it, posing as a house buyer inspecting a property over the road to get a better look at the street and an idea of the neighbours' daytime habits. He'd tracked and followed the guy too, and it was him that he pictured now. Ten minutes to go. That meant he'd be pulling up out the back of the St George Bank. He'd be loading the last of the bags and marking them off on the sheet in the front.

Michael thought over the workings of the van. When Adrian gave the all-clear, it was his job to approach and penetrate the vehicle as quickly as possible. It was imperative that no one see him do it. Once he was in, there were the alarms, the locks, getting all the money safely into the backpacks and the backpacks to the back of the van, where he needed to have the door ready to spring open when Adrian signalled that the car was in place, ready to go.

Adrian's job was easy: he only had to watch and wait while Peter went into the house, then signal Michael when he came back out again, so he sat thinking about how good it would be when they'd left the car in the Big W carpark and were safely on the train back to Sydney. They'd just look and be like ordinary backpackers, only they'd be rich, rich! And maybe the money would bring back some of what he'd lost these last two years. Maybe if he had money he wouldn't be so unhappy and that feeling that had started after Wendy's death would stop. Maybe he'd even be able to sleep at night again ... No, stop it, he told himself, he couldn't think about that, not now, not here; he had to remain focused. He'd begged Jeff for this chance. He couldn't let all the promises he'd made become lies.

But the ten minutes became five, two, then one, then the driver was five minutes late, ten.

'He's not coming.'

'Shut up, of course he's coming.'

'But the time? It's after twelve.'

'So what?'

'So he should be here.'

'So what do you suggest we do then? You want to leave?'

'No, I just think ...'

'You want to, you want to leave. Fuck! Why did you even come?'

'I never said I wanted to leave.' And Adrian hadn't thought it either; he was trying really hard not to think it, and indeed he felt more committed now than ever.

'Michael?' Peter demanded before Adrian could explain. 'I suppose you're chickening out too?'

'I'm not sure.'

'You're not sure about what? He's late, so what?'

'So I don't like this. I don't like surprises.'

'What? Come on, it's him, that's all.' Peter pointed at Adrian in the back seat. 'He's just made you nervous. Damn it, I told Jeff we needed a pro, not an amateur pimp who's been shut away brooding over some stupid girl for too long. Michael, trust me, everything is fine, we're gonna sit here until he comes and then we're going to do everything just like we planned. Right?'

'Maybe.'

'No, not maybe. Come on, both of you. We only get one shot at this and if we don't go through with it now Jeff will send another crew up next week and we'll get nothing. He won't give us a second go at it. How many security van drivers pop home for lunch with a van full of the bank's money for people like us to steal? No more after this, that's for sure, and it's either us or Jeff and another crew that make sure of that.' Peter looked first at Adrian, who hadn't needed any convincing anyway.

'Okay, you're right, I'm sorry, I ...' But Adrian had really wanted to say 'No, you stupid dick, why don't you just go and get ...' but it wasn't the right time and he'd already started shifting his focus back to Michael when a flash in the rear-vision mirror caught his eye. The white security van had rounded the corner and was slowing down for the speed bump just behind them. They all turned and tried not to look.

'Mike ...?' By now the van had pulled up outside number thirty-nine and the driver had got out and was locking the door. He paused for a moment as he took the key out of the lock, his eyes fixing on the car. They all tried to sink a little further back into the seat. He looked right at them a moment, but then went around the van and into the house. 'Mike?'

An hour later they were all sitting on the train heading back toward the city, but if things had gone to plan it sure didn't feel like it.

'What's wrong?' Peter finally asked. 'What is it? The job went fine.'

'I don't like it,' Michael answered.

Peter let out a sigh, looked out the window a moment, then picked up the bag and swung over to sit beside Adrian and in front of Michael. 'You don't like what?'

'It wasn't necessary.'

'What wasn't necessary?'

'Whatever you did in that house.'

'What, how did you ...?'

'Adrian.' Peter looked at Adrian, who sat up, surprised.

'But I didn't say ... I wouldn't I only thought ...'

'It was in his face when you picked me up in the car, and in your reply just now,' said Michael.

'What was?' Peter asked.

'Whatever it was you did.'

'What did I do?'

'I don't know, you tell me.'

Peter considered it a moment. 'And so what? What if I did do something? What does it matter?'

'It matters a lot.'

'Why, did you have a thing for him or something? Did you want to see him again?'

'It wasn't professional,' Michael insisted.

'So what?'

'And it ruined everything.'

'Why? We didn't get caught.'

'But we will.'

'How?'

'Because they'll find us, that's how. People forgive thieves, they root for them when they see them on the telly, they're like folk heroes. They let people believe that there's a way out of their stupid boring lives, a way to beat the system. Christ, they help them get away half the time. But not murderers, no way, everyone hates murderers. Even if you kill a bad person they'll hunt you down. Death takes away everything and people don't stop until they catch you.'

Peter sat back in the seat. 'But he needed to be shut up, he would have told, he would have ...'

'It was wrong,' said Michael. 'You were wrong. You could have tied him up and that would have been that, but you didn't. You did something you shouldn't have done, and you've screwed it up for all of us.'

'So what do we do?' Peter asked in a quieter, less assertive voice.

'I don't know, but not what we were going to do, that's for sure.'

'What, no, the plan ...' Peter protested.

'Screw the plan.'

'And Jeff? If we don't turn up with the money he'll come looking for us.'

'Forget Jeff. What's he got, five men, two he can spare? It's the cops we need to worry about now, they're the ones that are going to come after us, and they'll have twenty million people behind them.'

'So what do we do?' Peter repeated.

'We get off at the next three stations and go our own separate ways and never speak of this again.'

'But what if ...?'

'I nark?' Adrian spoke up. He'd seen the way Peter was looking at him and didn't want to hear the end of the question.

'It doesn't matter. It's still the best chance we have.'

'Then I get off first,' said Adrian. Michael considered the request. 'All right. You'll get off at the next stop, then me, then Peter.'

'But ...' Peter objected.

'But what?' answered Michael sharply, looking straight at him. 'You got us into this.'

Ten minutes later the train began to slow down for the next station and Adrian, watched carefully by Peter and Michael, stood in position ready to make his escape. He was happy to be getting off the train and out of this situation. Peter had never liked him and if he'd stayed much longer he might have started getting ideas into his head. Also, without giving the loot to Jeff's goons first he had more than three times the amount he'd expected to walk away with. And perhaps more importantly, now he'd be out on his own again. He didn't like being around other people lately, and especially not people like Peter.

When the train stopped, Adrian got off, walked out onto the platform, turned around, looked back, then disappeared behind the moving wall of people. The whistle blew, the doors were about to close ... they were half shut, closing, closing, then all of a sudden Adrian reappeared and stepped back onto the train.

'What happened? Why didn't you go?' Peter demanded, but he

could already see the answer out the window. Through the thinning crowd on the platform outside he could see three uniformed policeman by the exit, two standing back watching the people walk past and one leaning forward inspecting a passenger's open bag.

'They're stopping everyone further down the line. Someone got butchered in Newcastle – the armed offenders are out and everything.' A young man of about twenty-five was leaning over behind them to see out their window. 'Fair dinkum, mate,' he continued. 'Cops told me and everything. They're stopping everyone, reckon they're headed back to the city. Don't know why they think they'd come on the train, but – pretty stupid if you ask me.' He carried on down the corridor.

'I say we draw straws,' suggested Adrian when the stranger was out of earshot.

'Shut up you ...' Peter started.

'Wait,' Michael interrupted. 'We don't have time for any of that. Look, we're already on the outskirts of the city, and he's right, we don't all have to go down for this.'

'But I can't get caught. It's murder they'll do me for ...'

'That's the risk *you* took.'

'But you'll dob me in, both of you,' Peter said.

'Yes, if we're caught we'll tell the cops that it wasn't us that killed Jim.'

'But then if anyone's caught I'll be caught too. You said yourself that they wouldn't stop ...'

'That's still up to you.'

'How, how is that up to me?'

'You leave,' Michael said. 'Leave as soon as you get off the train.'

'Leave what?'

'The country.'

'The country?'

'Yes.'

'But my family ... my life ...?'

'Stop. It doesn't matter now. The more you keep to yourself from here on in, the better. Right now we need to co-operate, work together if any of us are to get out of this.'

'And there's no other way?'

'Not unless you can think of something in the next few seconds ... No? Then yes. There's no other way.'

'Okay, okay damn it, we'll draw straws,' Peter said.

'So the loser sits here and makes some sort of diversion while the other two make a run for it?' Adrian asked.

'Yes.'

'Where? When?'

'Central is probably our best bet. The cops can't stop everyone leaving there, especially not at this time of day – it'd be impossible.'

'And we don't admit to the murder?'

'No.'

'We tell them it was Peter.' In a way this pleased Adrian.

'Yes, if we have to, but that's all we tell them. When they ask we say it was an organised job, that we didn't know any more about the other two than their first names.'

'Like in *Reservoir Dogs*?'

'Exactly?'

'And Jeff?'

'Screw Jeff.'

'Then we're all agreed?' Adrian wanted to be sure.

'Yes.'

'And the money?'

'That doesn't change.'

'But why?' Peter objected. 'If the person staying is going to be caught anyway, why should we lose all that ...?'

'Because nothing's certain, and if the cops find it, it will give the other two more time to get away.'

'They could throw it into the crowd,' suggested Adrian. 'The people would go nuts.'

'Yes. If everything else failed, good thinking.'

Michael quickly fashioned three straws out of matches he took from his top pocket and held them out in front of them in his clenched fist.

'How do we know you haven't rigged it?' Peter asked.

'I'll take whichever is left is how.'

'Okay. Adrian, you first.'

Adrian leaned forward, picked out a match and pulled it from his fist. It was short. Peter's was longer and so was Michael's. Adrian sat staring at the match in disbelief. He wanted to say something meaningful, something cool, but instead he closed his fingers and clenched his fist in determination. He'd known it would be him.

'So what's the plan?' he asked.

Michael looked back at him, smiling. 'Good man. When the train stops and the doors open I want you to start making a noise, as much noise as you can. Yell like you've never yelled before. Make out like you're having a fit or something, whatever you've got to do. People will stop and look and the police will leave the exits and come running when they realise something's going on. Peter and I will gun it in opposite directions. Peter, you go out that door and I'll go out this one.' He indicated each end of the carriage. 'From then on it's every man for himself, okay?'

Had the trip gone on any longer Adrian might have been able to talk about a few of the good things he'd done as a free man. He might have even admitted to a few of the bad things too. But they were already on the Harbour Bridge and everything just seemed to be getting faster and faster as they hurtled through the city. All the commuters had filled the train now, too, and they all stood poised ready to gush out onto the platform at Central.

Right before the doors opened Adrian found himself

remembering the time he and Wendy had made out on one of the seats on the platform in the middle of the night. She was always so warm, and she'd had a power to help him make sense of everything, to keep him out of trouble. All his mates had said that she was boring, no fun, plain. But he'd never felt the same way or been so happy without her. And as the doors opened and he stood and started yelling like a madman and Peter and Michael rushed out onto the platform into the great current of people he found himself wondering, for what must have been the millionth time, what would have happened if he'd forgiven her, or at least hesitated before he pushed her.

FLIGHT 103

MATT WATCHED THE flight attendants wrestling with the lifejackets the passengers were to use should they find themselves plummetting to a fiery death. It was good to be heading home. He had been away a month and it would be great to see Amy again. If she was there. He had left in a hell of a huff and she had screamed that she never wanted to see him again. But that was the same old shit, wasn't it? The same old argument that went nowhere and did nothing. The last few months had been pretty bad. She had always been out or unhappy, and would never tell him why, never tell him what it was that hurt her, just that he made her feel bad. But maybe it would be different now. Maybe the time apart had solved many of the problems. He had found a whole heap of loneliness without her, and he could hardly wait to watch her undress again, no, tear off her clothes again, and make love to her over and over until exhaustion took away every little bit of pain.

The flight attendants finished their demonstration and started checking that everyone had their seatbelts on ready for take-off. One of them also said that because it was so early in the morning and many people would want to sleep on the flight, all the blinds must be shut until further notice. Another started closing the door, but a group of last-minute passengers arrived. Matt could hear them running up the tunnel toward the plane and he and everybody else leaned out of their seats trying to see who they were.

Matt felt uneasy as soon as he saw them. He watched the first ones walk down the aisle, looking quickly from one person to the next. They reminded him of Jews he had seen in a movie about the Holocaust searching a row of corpses for their loved ones – their white faces, their lost, blank, empty expressions.

Matt shifted even more uncomfortably in his seat. This was way too weird, way too strange. If he had been driving down a dark road he might have stopped and turned around, or had he been in a house that seemed to be telling him to get out he might have left to escape what he was feeling, but he was on a plane, and it wasn't possible, was it? He looked at the door and started fondling the seatbelt for the release button: maybe this would be his last chance. He clicked the button and started to stand up, but someone had stopped right in front of him. He knew who it was before he looked up.

'Amy, Amy I thought ...?'

She raised a finger to his lips and sat down beside him. 'I bet you thought lots of things.'

'But how ... what ...'

'Am I doing here?'

Matt looked at her. 'I came down here last week to visit my sister and I wanted to fly back sooner to meet you, but this was the first flight I could get and so here I am. Surprise!'

Matt was glad to see her but it didn't explain all the other people, and sister, what sister? He shrugged his shoulders. She was there now. Amy, right there in front of him. What else could matter?

'So are you mad at me?' he asked.

'No.'

'You?'

'What?'

'Are you mad at me?'

'No.'

'And did you miss me?' she asked.

'Yes.'

'And you?'

'Yes. Too much.'

'What, don't say that.'

'Why?'

'Because it's not nice.'

'But what if I missed you so much it just about drove me mad?'

'Then that's good.'

'Did you miss me?' he asked.

'Yes.'

'As much as me?'

'I don't know about that, you nut case.' She jabbed him in the stomach playfully.

'Hey,' he protested, grabbing her around the waist and bringing her down into his lap. They looked at each other more seriously.

'So,' he said, 'did you really miss me?'

But before she could answer another voice come over the speaker. 'Would all passengers be seated now? We're ready for take-off.'

Matt glanced up the aisle. He hadn't noticed the plane moving or even that the engines had started, but he could hear them now as they sped up and he quickly put Amy back into the seat beside him.

'And so,' she said, leaning over slightly and sliding her hand inside his shirt as the engines got even louder. 'You really been missing me, huh?'

He smiled. 'Oh yeah.'

Matt took his seatbelt off as soon as he could, pulled Amy back onto his lap and started kissing her and whispering more private things into her ear. He wanted to do things with her right then and there; he couldn't see anything but her. It was as if all his questions were answered, as if all his uncertainty and fear had been taken away, and he wanted her more now than he had ever wanted anyone or anything. But she kept saying no to the sex. He suggested ways it could be done. No. He became more and more creative; still no. He suggested the toilet. No again. He could hardly handle it, he was so excited. He looked around the cabin for more inspiration ... but hold on. Wait. He pushed Amy off and sat up.

'Matt, what is it? What is it?' she asked. 'You've gone all white.'

He stood up to get a better look at what was going on around him. No one was talking. All of them were kissing or cuddling. What the hell was going on here?

'Right,' he said, sitting down again. 'The truth?'

'What, what do you mean the truth? What about?'

'I mean why are you here? Why are all of these people here? And why did you all arrive together like that? What's going on?'

'Nothing, Matt, nothing's going on.'

He thought for a moment. 'Who gave you the ticket?'

'I told you, I was at my sister's and ...'

'No, you didn't have the money, we didn't have the money, remember. That was half the problem to begin with. No, who paid for the trip. Who bought you the ticket for this flight?'

She was about to protest but stopped. A change came over her face. 'I wasn't meant to say.'

'Who, who told you not to say?'

'They did.'

'Who is they?'

'The men from your work.'

'What men?'

'They came around last week. They wanted me to come up here and surprise you. They said I could go to my sister's in Chicago and then meet up with you on the way back. They said it was like a reward, a promotion thing because you've been working so hard.'

'And you didn't talk to the other people before you came on the plane?'

'No.'

'And these men, what did they look like?'

'Why, what does it matter?' Matt was silent. 'Matt, you're scaring me.'

'Because I left Anderson and Davis a month ago. That's half the reason I went away. I've been looking for a new job. I didn't want to tell you until I got one.'

'Oh,' she said mildly, then 'Oh!' when significance had had a chance to take hold. 'So what ...?'

'I don't know,' Matt said quietly, looking around again. 'But I don't like it.'

'What's going to happen? What are they doing to do?' she asked, taking his hand.

The flight attendants began to gather at the front of the cabin. Matt and Amy watched them carefully. They were talking quietly, and all looking at something one of them was holding. Amy moved around trying to see what it was.

'It's a video camera.'

'So they're going to film it then,' said Matt quietly.

'Film what?'

'Whatever it is they're going to do,' he replied.

Amy grabbed him tighter. Nobody else seemed to have noticed what was going on, but then the largest of the men stood right at the front of the cabin where everybody could see him and took off his white uniform to reveal a green one, complete with a munitions belt from which he took a shiny black gun. This managed to catch everyone's attention. Someone screamed, then someone else. A young woman tried to jump out of her seat but was knocked back down by one of the attendants who had also taken off his uniform. The girl's boyfriend tried to intervene, but sat back down quickly when the guard put the barrel of his gun hard against his forehead. The man at the front waited until the cabin was silent again.

'I am Nutious Claiborne and as you can see my men and I have taken over this plane.' He paused for a moment, looking around as if allowing people time to object, before he continued. 'For many years your country has brought us death and starvation. It has taken food from our mothers' mouths and crammed our children's minds with fear, stealing their future with its economic sanctions and western re-education. You have heard about this on your radios, read about it in your newspapers and seen it on your televisions, all the time thinking that it was never your problem ... Well, today my men and I are here to make sure that you, your president and all the people in your county know that it is your problem. Today you are all going to learn what it means to face death. Today you are going to learn what it's like to really feel fear.'

Matt observed that he seemed to be talking more into the camera than to the passengers and, when he had finished, his exit from the cabin was definitely more for the camera than them. He came back in after a couple of seconds to have a brief, whispered conversation with one of the guards.

'One of my men,' he continued a few seconds later, 'has informed me that in light of certain recent world events some of you might take it upon yourselves to put your own lives and the lives of my men at risk by trying to overthrow our command. Do so and you will die, and all your families will die too, just as our people all die when you steal our oil, enslave our people and bomb our land. So please, as you can see,' he lifted his hand, gesturing at all the people, 'we know all about your lives. We know where you and every other member of your family lives and we have people in place who will kill them if you cross us.' He disappeared again, leaving four of the six men to stand guard.

'I didn't know Matt, I swear,' Amy started. 'They came around, I didn't even want to let them in at first, but they had money, a cash bonus they said and I believed them. I'm sorry, Matt, I'm so sorry.'

Part of Matt did want to blame her, but he found it hard to be angry and instead pulled her close. 'It's all right,' he said. 'You couldn't have known. Why would you? Really, Amy, look at me, it's all right ...'

Matt glanced around the cabin again. Everyone seemed as shocked as they were. What was going to happen? Were they really going to die?

Amy seemed to read his thoughts. 'We're going to die, aren't we?'

'I don't know.' She raised an eyebrow. 'I mean, how do we really know?' he continued.

'Because he said ...'

'Yes, but they want us to co-operate,' Matt replied.

'So?'

'Well why?'

'Why?'

'Yes, why would they want us to co-operate?'

'What do you mean?'

'Well, it's more like ...'

'More like what?'

'Well, it's more like they want us to perform,' Matt said.

'Yes, so they can make their sick video.'

'Yes, but why, why do they want to make a video?' he asked.

'So they can show the world how weak and vulnerable we all are.'

'Yes, but what I mean is, how are they going to show the world? If they're going to crash the plane then they'll die too. How are they going to show the world?'

'By phone – they could be sending the images as they're taken. They seem pretty organised.'

'Maybe, but then why do they want us to perform?'

Amy looked at him, puzzled. She didn't really see what he was getting at. 'I don't understand,' she said.

'Neither do I. But there's something strange about it. Something that doesn't add up. Like if they're going to kill us, if they're going to scare us, why don't they film that? Why all the drama, all the theatrics?'

But a fight had already broken out. A large man had rushed one of the guards, only to be pushed back and shot in the stomach for his trouble. He fell down in the aisle to yells of hysteria from the other passengers. Another such attack followed, and another, until a hush filled the whole cabin. Amy was shaking now, and she grasped Matt tightly.

'We're going to die.' Matt had started to believe it now too.

In answer to the outbursts, though, and perhaps to further torment their captives, the terrorists were relaying images from the cockpit onto the central screen at the front of the cabin. Everyone tried not to look at it, but it was hard to take your eyes off it. The plane was descending into a large canyon, flying very close to the rocks on either side. People were screaming and crying now. Some were on their knees praying. Some were lying on the floor.

And now they were heading straight for a giant rocky outcrop in the canyon. The screams were getting louder and louder, everyone was going crazy. The lights in the cabin began to click on and off. They were getting closer, the screams were getting louder, louder. Matt could hardly hear himself think. Amy was groping him, her frightened hands like claws, and he touched her too. Were these to be their last few seconds? Those rocks were too close now, there was no time to turn ... they were going to hit, they were going to hit ...

The screen went to static. Matt opened his eyes quickly. All the hijackers but the one with the camera were gone, and even he now seemed to be backing out of the cabin. Matt leaned out of the seat to see where he was going and could hardly believe it. The door to the outside was open! Suddenly it all made sense. He leaned over to the window and pulled up the blind. It seemed impossible but they were still on the ground. They had never taken off at all. Matt looked at Amy. She took his hand and stood up. It was time to go home.

After Midnight

DONNIE AND CAT

'HEY COME QUICK, it's begun.' Cat put her book aside and walked over to the window. In the usually quiet streets below people were moving around in the early evening. Some walked back from the shops with armfuls of food, others loaded cars, trailers, vans and trucks with clothes and water and blankets, furniture and even fridges. They seemed tense, nervous. She didn't like the looks on their faces. They didn't seem like her neighbours any more. All the friendliness had gone. She moved closer to Donnie.

'They're scared, aren't they?' she said.

'Yes.'

'So am I.' He pulled her in tight to him. 'Will we be all right?'

'Yes.'

'What if we wait too long?'

Donnie didn't answer, but the question had been in his mind. They'd packed their bags three days ago, but he didn't want to leave yet. It wouldn't be safe. If people saw them going they might leave too and a panic could start. No, they must be responsible and wait like everybody else. And yet, he reminded himself, unlike the others they would have an advantage. The people outside were all expecting to use the roads, but if the bombs came that would be impossible. It was nearly 30 kilometres to get to the outskirts of Sydney from the city, and if four million people all frightened for their lives tried to use the same two or three roads at once it just wouldn't work. It would take an orderly, controlled procession of cars a week to evacuate the city. Anyone who had driven in rush-hour traffic could figure that out.

There was hope, too, he kept trying to remind himself. If the bombs came they would take at least three hours to arrive and both of them were fit enough to cover maybe 10 kilometres an hour. They would jog directly west, out through the suburbs and into the bush and from then on, who knew? Who knew anything in this strange time?

Donnie stepped back from the window and closed the curtain. Cat smiled weakly. She trusted him and he appreciated it.

'How's your book going?' he asked.

'I'm just at a really good bit.' He liked how she could escape reality like this. She was wise for her thirty-two years, intelligent too, yet she had a type of sweet innocence that he loved. He held her for a moment, then stepped back.

'We'd better have a quick look at the news.'

'You're going to turn the TV on again?'

'Yes, just for a moment.'

Cat returned to the couch but did not open her book. Donnie pressed the remote and reached over for her hand.

The crisis had begun two years before. Right when the integrity and sustainability of the oil fields in the Middle East were beginning to be seriously questioned, the unthinkable happened. China discovered the largest oil field ever found, less than ten kilometres from its coast. The Americans were visibly upset. It was even rumoured that within an hour of the announcement their ships were headed toward Chinese waters. But their surprise attack was foiled by the United Nations, who were quick to publicly condemn any act of aggression and to offer full support to the new world power. The United States was beaten before it had begun and its people were angry. Many started to question the integrity of their red-faced president, who had had a troubled relationship with the Chinese throughout his first term in office. Tension grew. The pressure increased and, aware of the threat, the Chinese quickly moved to increase their arsenal, purchasing nuclear weapons regardless of price from the former Soviet Union to the north and India to the south. America called for allies and, among others, Australia answered. Talks began. America demanded an immediate stop to China's purchases of weapons of mass destruction. China did not comply. Talks broke down and, under increased pressure from the American people, the president issued an ultimatum: they either ceased their 'illegal' activities within three days or faced the consequences. Weapons were pointed and the world, and Donnie and Cat shut up in their Glebe flat in the inner west of Sydney, waited.

Cat watched the news again for a moment. It was the same interview with the American president from yesterday, followed by the same interview with the Chinese from the day before, so she picked up her book and started reading again. Donnie kept watching. He still couldn't believe it. All his life he had been partly interested in politics and completely interested in human nature – and the correlation between the two. And indeed this whole problem was no more complex than any collision of ego and pride that might occur within any single person or relationship, yet it seemed to completely lack any rationality.

It was so simple. The Americans were used to power and now they couldn't have it any more. It was being taken away from them, not purposely, perhaps not even vindictively, and they couldn't accept it. Now they were even threatening to destroy what they wanted so no one could have it. Donnie clenched his fist and banged it on the side of his chair. Why? What did it matter? Australia would still be Australia, the land still the land, the sea still blue, no matter who controlled the world. Cat squeezed Donnie's hand, and he tried to smile back at her. In a way, he wasn't as brave as her, even if he had to pretend to be.

A sudden flash came over the TV. A newsreader's face appeared on the screen. His hair was ruffled and someone was still struggling to pin a microphone to his shirt. Cat and Donnie sat up straighter. The newsreader's voice was slow; he was trying to be calm. He tried not to break eye contact with the camera. 'Australia. Channel Ten has just received a report that America has launched a nuclear strike against China and that China has answered!'

Cat turned to Donnie. 'The bombs are coming. They're really coming, they've really done it, I can't believe ...'

'Wait,' Donnie said quickly. 'There's more.' He had to know when and where. They might not even have launched anything against Australia.

'There have been reports of two sets of missiles, launched ten minutes apart, headed toward both Sydney and Melbourne and at their current speed they will be here in a little over three hours. So please, Channel Ten advises that you leave both these cities as quickly and as calmly as possible ...' The reporter waited a moment, glanced at someone else in the newsroom, nodded, then looked back at the camera. 'This will be Channel Ten's last report this evening, but I am told it will be put on repeat. Goodbye and good luck.' He stood and rushed from sight.

AFTER MIDNIGHT 149

Donnie and Cat could hear the noise outside already as panic filled the air. People yelled, engines revved, horns had already started tooting. The curtain had been raised.

A couple of minutes later Cat and Donnie were downstairs with their packs. Donnie looked at his watch. 'It's almost nine. We have until just after midnight.' He put his hands on her shoulders and looked into her eyes. 'We have to move fast, okay?'

She smiled.

'But we'll be all right,' he said in the most reassuring voice he could find. 'Is your pack okay? It's not too heavy?'

She shook her head.

'And is it tight? It needs to be tight so it doesn't bounce too much and hurt you or come loose.' He pulled at it, making sure there was no slack.

'It's okay,' she said, still trying to smile.

Donnie tested his own bag. There was a lot in it and he wondered again if he'd taken too much. He had packed thermals, matches, water, some food, a torch, a knife, some spare clothes, soap, a compass, a blanket. What else could they leave behind? They might need it all. Cat had wanted to take other stuff as well, valuables and family heirlooms, but Donnie had told her that a lot of people would die for their cars and their homes and their precious things. 'Leaving everything we can behind is our best hope. We have to travel light.'

'We'll be okay,' he said again. 'I promise. Here ...' He picked up a retractable dog leash up from beside the door and attached one end to his belt and the other to her bag strap. 'This goes up to ten metres. We have to stay close together no matter what, okay?' She nodded again and he kissed her one last time.

'You might panic and want to run faster,' Donnie had told Cat. 'But we can't. We will burn out too fast and we have to be able to keep going. And' – he'd stressed this several times – 'whatever you do, don't look at people. There'll be many distractions, things we'll have never seen and many more we might never imagine, but we can't give in to them. Keep your head down and concentrate on your breathing, and whatever happens try to stay calm.'

Cat had understood this too and assumed it wouldn't be a problem, but right away it proved harder than she thought. There were people everywhere and they were all doing strange and extraordinary things. Some were angry and fighting. A lot were stuck in long lines of tooting cars banging their steering wheels and yelling in frustration. Some even got out and attacked other people before they could get out of their seats. This was bad on the smaller roads where the traffic only seemed to move every now and then, but was absolutely unbelievable on the larger roads.

Cat kept feeling the tug of her husband as the line between them reached its full length and every time she reminded herself to remain focused and not lag behind, but it was so hard. There was so much to see. The intensity in the air was incredible too. The world seemed so different. A couple of times she tried to catch up with Donnie and stay at his side, but then something new and even more amazing would grab her attention and she would fall back and feel the tug. She tried again and again to focus on her breathing.

Donnie was being distracted, too. He kept thinking of the road ahead and of how much time they had. Two bombs were on their way. The first would be exploded at high altitude to throw out all navigation and communications. The flash would be bright and the shock wave powerful enough to knock you over if you got in its way, but it wouldn't destroy much. The second one would be the killer. A Russian-made bomb probably. An intercontinental ballistic missile with a fantastically high-yield nuclear warhead. Probably ten or twenty thousand megatons, set to detonate at low altitude. The initial blast would completely level the CBD and inner suburbs and he figured they'd better be at least 20 kilometres away and under cover when it went off. He wondered a few times as they ran if they should have brought bikes, but when he saw two men chasing another to take his bike from him he was glad they hadn't. It was better, too, that they could change direction quickly and get past anything that got in their way.

He glanced at his watch. They had been running for half an hour and were in Leichhardt now. His breathing was steady and Cat was keeping up behind him. They were making good time. In another half an hour they would have a chance of surviving the initial blast. The back streets they were choosing were mostly empty. Some cars were trying to weave their way through suburbia, but the main roads were too many and too busy to drive across, so they weren't getting that far. A few people saw Donnie and Cat and yelled things after them; one even gave chase, but something else grabbed his attention before he caught up. After Five Dock Donnie tried to keep them as close to the water as he could. A lot of people lived near the water around Sydney, but they would only be moving away from there so it was probably the least populated now.

They were well clear of the CBD now, and making very good time too. Things might be just be okay, if they kept going. After Parramatta they crossed a main road full of people even angrier and more frustrated than before. Some were ramming other cars out of the way and one even got pushed right off the side of a bridge and smashed onto the cars on the road below. It was hard not to look and Donnie was glad when they'd crossed the road and started zigzagging their way through the quieter suburban streets.

When he suddenly felt a large tug at his waist he stopped and turned around. 'Cat, what are you doing? We can't stop. We have to keep ...'

Her face was frozen and she did not seem to be able to hear him.

'Cat, what is it?' He walked back to her and turned to see what she was looking at. In the front window of a house the face of a young girl was looking back at them.

'We can't leave her,' Cat said.

Donnie thought for a moment and looked back down the street. He really wanted to keep going right now, damn it. Why did she have to look around? He took a big breath. There was no point in getting angry now. 'What about her parents?'

'What about them? She'll be dead in an hour if we leave her.'

Donnie wanted to explain that it was dangerous to go into the house, that her parents might be crazy with panic and do who knows what if they thought they were taking their little girl, but it was obvious that Cat wouldn't budge unless they did.

'Okay, let's go and get her then.' He looked up. The girl was smiling at them now. Apparently she had understood their conversation. She met them at the front door.

'We have to leave,' Cat said plainly. 'And you have to come with us. It is important. We have no time to explain now. Do you understand? Is that okay?' The little girl nodded. She had a smile on her face but tears had come into her eyes. Cat glanced at Donnie. 'Your parents have gone, haven't they?' The child nodded again.

'What's your name?' Donnie said.

'Rachel.'

'Hi Rachel. I'm Cat and this is Donnie. Now Rachel. Have you got a jacket?' She nodded. 'Good. Now what I want you to do is run inside and grab it as fast as you can – quick, quick.' Donnie looked at his watch.

'I'll carry her if she slows us down,' said Cat.

'I didn't mean ... I'm sorry. Look, it's nothing to do with her or you ...'

'No, I know, and you're right. We need to hurry. Come on, Rachel, I want you to hop on my back, we have to run now.'

They ran another block but Donnie had to stop twice to let them catch up. He looked at his watch again. If they hurried they could still make it to the water at Rooty Hill, about five kilometres away. He rushed to Cat, grabbed the girl and started running with her in his arms.

MALCOLM

Earlier that day, Malcolm Baxter sat at his desk in Canberra deep in thought. Had he made the right decision? Had he done the right thing? Maybe he would never know. Maybe that would be his sentence, to live on in darkness and doubt, with no chance of redemption or for a clear answer. He turned to the window. Canberra was still quiet. The people were nervous, but there was none of the hysteria expected in Sydney or Melbourne where the bombs would strike if it came to that. He tried to imagine them in downtown Sydney. All those people that worked in those high-rise buildings and little coffee shops. The news reported that the city was running as normal and people weren't leaving, but they must be scared.

He tried to bring his mind back to the present, to Canberra, to his wife and family. They were safe, thank God, and yet – he bit down hard on his pen – what did that say about him? He'd told the people in his national address not two hours ago that America and China would never engage in a worldwide nuclear war, that he believed and trusted that the presidents of both countries would resume negotiations through diplomatic channels before the mandate expired. But if he believed that, why hadn't he answered his critics and gone to Sydney himself? He started pacing again. There was a knock at the door.

'Sir?'

'Yes.'

'Your wife is on the phone.' Malcolm picked up the receiver and pressed the button for line one.

'Michelle, what is it?'

'Malcolm, I'm worried.' Before he could answer, there was another knock and his deputy prime minister, Roger Harrison, walked in.

'Michelle, I'll call you as soon as I can.'

He put down the phone.

'Roger?'

'A group of protesters in Martin Place is growing too big and getting out of control and there's fears they might start a panic in Sydney. I've just met with the National Guard, they say they could use tear gas and ...'

'No.'

'Prime Minister?'

'No. I want to go there myself.'

'But sir, what about your family? Sir, if they attack what about your country?'

Malcolm looked the other man squarely in the eyes and for the first time in many days said something he actually believed. 'Those people are my country.'

An hour later the prime minister's helicopter and its escort landed on the wharf in Sydney and between two police escorts Malcolm travelled in a big black car up to Martin Place. He had sent his white-faced deputy south to Melbourne where it was reported a similar group was growing in size near Flinders Street station.

When he pulled up, press swamped the car. It was the first time they'd been allowed near him in days and the questions came thick and fast, too many to hear or comprehend. Malcolm waited for the buzz to die down before he answered any questions.

'Prime Minister,' began a reporter from Channel Seven. 'Will there be a war?' 'Prime Minister, Prime Minister, will they bomb Sydney first or Melbourne?'

Finally he managed to speak. 'I wait today just as we all must wait. I don't know what action the Americans will take to enforce their mandate on the Chinese if they don't receive an answer in time. However, it's still my hope, as the hours come to an end, as I'm sure it's the hope of many of my fellow Australians who remain confident in our support of the United States, that the matter will be resolved peacefully and without the use of force. And in more direct answer to many of your questions, to demonstrate my confidence in a peaceful solution and to offer further reassurance to the people of Australia, I will not return to Canberra but stay here in the city until such time as the peaceful road to that solution has been resumed. So please stay calm and continue as normal.'

Later in the day, Malcolm and an entourage of twenty ministers, advisers and bodyguards took up residence in the penthouse suite of a government-run building on the North Shore, overlooking the harbour and Sydney city. The air in the room was tense and everyone was growing increasingly nervous. Telephones rang constantly as Malcolm talked to American diplomats and ministers as well as the leaders of other countries that also had missiles pointed in their direction. Through a satellite link he addressed the nation again at five o'clock, saying that, although talks had not been resumed or the mandate lifted, there was still hope of a peaceful solution. But then the announcement came: the missiles had been aimed and fired, and by midnight they would be here.

Within minutes the first helicopter landed on the roof just above them and took the first and largest group of people away. Malcolm was too stunned to speak. One of the security men had to take him by the arm and lift him up when his own chopper arrived a few minutes later.

'Prime Minister.' Malcolm looked up at the man. 'We have to go.'

He nodded and let the man lead him up onto the roof. There were only six of them left now. The others, uncertain of a place in the helicopters, must have chanced a spot in the bunkers below. Malcolm started to get in through the helicopter's open door, but stopped and stood back.

'Sir?' The guard looked at him again.

Malcolm looked into his face and then out over the roof to the harbour bridge where the two Australian flags at its summit were lifting and moving slightly in the evening breeze. He stood back. 'I'm not leaving.'

'Sir?'

'No. Go. I'm not coming.'

'But, sir. You must. We have to get you to a safe place.'

'No. Give me your radio. There's work to be done.'

'Sir?'

'Shelters? Where are the shelters? Who's opening them? Who's in charge?'

Malcolm was soon back downstairs, co-ordinating the bomb shelters via the radio to the National Guard, and sending off his helicopter and the security guards to use the loudspeaker to direct people to safety. Each time it came back the guards told Malcolm that this must be their last trip, that they had to be clear of the city and on the ground well before the bomb exploded, but Malcolm refused to leave, even when one of the guards told him the pilot was beginning to say he might not come back. After the fifth trip he didn't, and Malcolm was left alone.

He stayed at the radio until the signal faded when the people at the other end were behind the closed doors of the shelters. What now? Should he leave? It would be almost impossible to get out of the city now. And yet what about Michelle, and Cathy his daughter? Didn't he owe it to them to at least try? He took his coat and left the room. Outside it was worse than he'd imagined. It was hopeless. He went back upstairs and found a bottle of brandy. He would sit beside the water, drink a toast to his wife, his daughter and his country, and watch the show.

SHANE

Shane Kelly had been in love with yachts and the water ever since he was a kid and his parents had had a little trailer-sailer called *Smithy*. He'd loved being in the little cabin. In large spaces he'd always felt a little uncomfortable, somehow, as if something might creep up on him when he had his back turned. He'd always wanted to live on a yacht, but had never imagined that he would be able to afford one. Then someone up north told him about an auction run by Waterways in Sydney. Apparently they auctioned off unregistered boats they found in the harbour, and without a reserve they sometimes went for as little as six or seven hundred dollars. Shane had been on the dole at the time and didn't have any money to speak of, but he hitchhiked down to Sydney to find out more. He was impressed. All he needed was the money. He tried to think of someone who might lend it to him; he even made a few phone calls and visited the bank, but all the answers were no. Disheartened, he spent his last few dollars on some food and beer, sat in the sun and got drunk and fell asleep on the grass at Circular Quay.

When he woke up, he lay staring over at the harbour bridge. He could see tourists walking over the great arch high above. He had seen the promos for the bridge climb and wondered how much they must make a day taking groups over it ten at a time. If only he could have their profits for a day – even for an hour. Then he could buy ten yachts. He looked away, then suddenly turned back. People were walking across the deck, too, on the footpath – that was half as high and totally free. He sat up and looked in his wallet. He had two dollars left.

An hour later he had found an internet café with cheap printing, made a sign and printed out ten copies.

Harbour Bridge Tours
$20 (including GST)
Phone Shane: 0431 837 855

He put them all up on backpacker notice boards in hostels around the city, then went to the library, put his cellphone on charge on an out-of-the-way power point and collected all the books he could find about the harbour bridge. By five o'clock he got his first call, and then three more before seven. The next day he met six people at Circular Quay, and gave them a walking tour of the harbour bridge. The second day he took twenty people around the bridge, and then on the third day thirty.

The following week he stopped taking calls and bought his yacht, a little 22-foot red jacket with a drop keel and full set of sails, and he quickly settled into an easy life of learning to sail and doing some light renovation in Lane Cove, where he'd paid cash for a mooring. It was nice not having to worry about anything more than what to have for dinner and how many more AC/DC albums the batteries in the stereo would last through. But then the trouble started.

Shane didn't watch or listen to the news, but on the day the bomb dropped he didn't have to to know something was wrong. He could feel it in the air. Curious, he rowed the dinghy ashore and went up onto the main street. What was going on? Everyone seemed to be in some kind of frenzy. He tried to talk to some of them but no one would stop. They all seemed to be heading into the supermarket, and those coming out had trolleys chock-a-block with food. He followed them in. The place was fuller than he'd ever seen it before and a lot of the shelves were nearly empty. He decided to get food too, and after an hour managed to get through the checkout with three full bags.

Back on the boat he stowed it all away then sat back up in the cockpit with a beer, watching the people on shore. Things seemed to be getting worse. It was dark now but maybe he should leave? He could go back and visit people up the north coast. No one up there had seen the boat yet, and he had a pretty good handle on sailing now. He thought about it a while longer, looked again at the people, in their cars now, all racing out onto the road, and finished his beer. 'Yeah, screw this.' He put on his favourite album and cast off.

At first he went slowly, but as he travelled around the bays and closer to the city the madness in the air seemed to get worse and he found himself slowly increasing the revs on the little outboard motor. There were some other boats on the harbour now, too, but they weren't the usual kind of 'wave at you and say hello' rich boatie types; some even cut him off to pass him. They were leaving too. What the hell was going on? When he approached the harbour bridge and the CBD there were more boats and they seemed even more reckless, so he steered right over to the left to keep out of their way. He was just under the bridge and near the shore when by chance he saw someone who looked familiar on the grass beside the water. Could it be? He went below to get the binoculars and have a better look. Yes, it was. He put the boat up beside a nearby jetty and helped the drunken man aboard.

SHANE AND MALCOLM

When they were well out of the harbour and off the coast, Shane pointed the boat north and tied the tiller to each side of the cockpit to keep them going straight, then went down into the cabin. Perhaps a cup of coffee would cheer up his famous guest, who hadn't yet said a word. There wouldn't be much room in here with two of them: there were only two small berths and a kind of half-V berth at the front that had sails on it. He cleared what he could off the second berth so his guest could use it as a seat, or a bed later, if he wanted. He smiled. It sure wouldn't be anything like he was used to.

The pot of water on the stove came to the boil and he poured two cups of coffee, then went back up the steps and sat down in the cockpit opposite Malcolm. He still seemed to be in some kind of stupor. It was colder up here now and darker away from the city. Malcolm's hands wrapped around the cup and after a moment he looked up.

'Bit of a strange day, huh?' Shane offered, taking a sip of coffee. 'People were acting really weird in the city. I'm bloody pleased to get out of there.'

'You're bloody lucky to have got out.'

'What do you mean?' Shane asked, happy to finally hear his guest talk.

Malcolm looked at him, then looked around the boat. 'You don't know what's going on, do you?' Shane shook his head. 'You don't go out much?'

'Nope, I like to keep to myself, be my own boss and that sort of thing – a bit like you.'

Malcolm gave a thin smile. 'So you know who I am?'

'Yeah, of course. I'm not that much of a hermit.'

They were silent for a moment before Malcolm spoke again. 'But you're wrong. A man like me can never be his own boss.'

'But you run the country. You *are* the boss!' Shane protested.

'Yes,' Malcolm said grimly. 'I did do that, but tell me, on this boat who really runs who?'

Shane puzzled. He was the boss, of course he was the boss. But when he thought for a moment realised he might understand. 'You mean there's always the wind and the rain?'

The prime minister nodded and seemed now to be smiling slightly. 'So you really don't know what's going on?'

'Well, I'm not stupid, I know there's something going on. All the people in town were acting crazy, and there were lines for everything. There was a really funny vibe in the air, too – I didn't like it at all. So I decided to split. That's when I saw you.'

'So why did you stop?'

'I don't know. When I first saw you I just thought, wow, this day is getting stranger and stranger, but when I got up closer you looked so lonely, or lost or forgotten or something. And seeing as everyone else seemed to be leaving in such a big hurry I thought maybe I should take you out of there as well. I guess I thought maybe you'd missed your ride or something, so I stopped. Is that all right?'

Malcolm smiled. He'd drunk most of the coffee now and had evidently sobered up a little. 'Yes. That's all right.' He reached out his hand to Shane.

'Oh, Shane Kelly.'

'Malcolm Baxter. Pleased to met you, Shane.'

'So what's going on, then?'

Malcolm explained to Shane in some detail the events of the last few weeks. 'So let me get this straight, you're telling me that everyone is splitting Sydney 'cause there's a nuclear bomb on its way from China?'

'Yes.'

'Bloody hell.'

'Yes.' The full magnitude of the situation took a few moments to settle on Shane. 'Bloody hell.' He repeated it two or three times.

'Yes,' Malcolm answered.

'Unreal.'

'Yes.'

'All those people.'

'Yes,' said Malcolm softly.

'Well, it's a good thing I got you then, isn't it?' Shane said finally.

Malcolm did not answer.

Shane went back down below, put the cups away and then sat on the bed. How strange and wonderful that there should be a nuclear bomb and he should meet Malcolm Baxter and that he would be his guest. He stared out the little window at the waves, then went back up to the cockpit and stood in front of the prime minister.

'So what are we going to do now?'

Malcolm's face did not change and all of a sudden Shane liked the whole thing a lot less. If there was no Sydney then what else would there not be? He had never really liked the city that much, and he didn't have any friends or relatives there, but he was still aware of its importance to Australia. They made beer there, for one thing. He was about to make a joke about having to drink Victoria Bitter when he stopped. 'What about your family? Are they in Sydney?'

'No. They're safe in Canberra.'

'Okay,' said Shane, standing up. 'Then that's where we will go.'

'But we're on a boat.'

'Yes, so we can sail south to Batemans Bay. Canberra is less than an hour from the coast down there. We'll go ashore and find a car or something.'

'You would do that? Is it possible? On this boat?'

'Well, the boat can do it, it can do anything, and I haven't got nothing else to do, so yeah, let's do it. We'll crank up the sails and let it rip. We could be down there in just a few days if we get a move on.'

'A few days?'

'Well, yeah. It's a couple of hundred kilometres.' Shane could see Malcolm's enthusiasm deflating. 'They'll be okay, won't they? They'll be safe where they are? There'll be people protecting them and that?' Malcolm looked at him. 'Yeah, sure they will be. Come on. Let's crank it up and get moving. You ever sailed before?' Malcolm shook his head. 'No? Well then you're going to have to put everything else out of your head now 'cause I'm going to need all of your attention. You've got a lot to learn.' Malcolm smiled.

'Okay?' Shane asked.

'Okay,' he agreed.

They sailed deep into the night. Malcolm liked this kind of work. In Canberra he had a Model T ford he had spent two years restoring in his workshop. He'd bought a Chevy Impala, too, that he'd started working on right before the election campaign seven years ago, but he hadn't been out to work on it much since – once on Christmas Day three years ago and another time just for a publicity shoot. He missed it, too. Work like this was good. It got you moving and breathing and cleared your mind. Later Malcolm started to feel really tired, but he didn't want to sleep yet, so instead he asked Shane for a big strong cup of coffee before he went to bed.

'All right,' he answered, smiling. 'So I guess it's about time I showed you the kitchen then.'

The kitchen was just a couple of cupboards, a little gas stove, a tiny little sink with a hand-held pump for the water and a place to hunch over while you waited as the roof in the cabin wasn't quite high enough to stand in.

After he had been given the grand tour and made his own cup of coffee, Malcolm sat at the tiller steering the boat and occasionally trimming the sails in the slight wind long after Shane had gone to bed below. He felt all right now, sober at least. The cool breeze on his face helped. There was no way he could have gone to sleep. The ghosts of the last few days were lurking too closely around him. He could feel them not far off in the darkness and they would be too much for closed eyes.

DONNIE AND CAT

The first flash came, followed by a noise so loud it sounded as though they were in the middle of a thousand thunderstorms. 'We have to run really fast now – everything we've got. Come on!' yelled Donnie and they broke into a sprint. The people were fewer now but the ones they saw were mad with panic. Some had wet their pants in the street. Donnie tried to keep as far away from them as possible. He looked down at his watch. It had been nearly ten minutes since the first blast. 'Move, move, move ...' he yelled. Rachel started crying. He could see the water now and they had to make it. They gave it absolutely everything and made it into the sea, panting for breath.

'There'll be a big flash and I want you to both take the biggest breath you can, then come down into the water with me and stay down for as long as you can. I'll hold your hands. Okay?' They both nodded. Donnie pulled them down to where their heads just stuck out of the water and closed his eyes. A few moments passed, then, just after midnight, the flash came and he pulled them down. There was a terrible noise, even louder than the one before. They waited for as long as they could.

'We made it, didn't we?' Cat said, dripping wet on the edge of the water. Rachel was smiling up at him, still clutching his hand.

'Yes, I think we made it.'

'But we have a long way to go yet, don't we?' she said half to Rachel and half to him.

'Yes,' he said, crouching down and holding Rachel's hand tight in his own and looking into her little face. 'But we don't have to run any more.'

The air was thick and smoky now. It stank of ash and soot and something else Donnie tried not to imagine. Everything in the streets was out of place – rubbish and plants and everything that wasn't held down lay on the road and across lawns and driveways. Wheelbarrows, clothes, tin, tools, shoes, dolls, plates ... it looked like a tip. Toward the city everything was black with dust and fumes that seemed to get thicker and spread as they watched. 'That air will be poisonous to breathe. We have to keep going. Come on.'

It was time for the second part of his plan. They walked quickly back into the suburbs and he started disappearing down driveways, leaving them on the road. After about twenty minutes he found what he was looking for and yelled for them to come. They found him on a back porch with a knife in his hand.

'What are you doing?' Cat asked as he started to slash the plastic cover of something.

'We need to move quickly now. That black cloud could be here in minutes if the wind changes.'

'But what about the magnetic pulse?' Donnie had explained this to her as another reason why they shouldn't try to leave in a car. A nuclear explosion created a huge magnetic pulse that destroyed everything electrical for hundreds of kilometres. That was why they fired the first one – to take out their enemy's communication systems. Otherwise the second bomb might be destroyed in the air before it reached its target.

'This wasn't running,' he said, winking at Rachel. They stood back as he finally ripped the cover right off the big dirt bike. 'And it will take us across country.'

'But how will you start it?' she asked nervously, looking into the house as if expecting someone to catch them stealing the motor cycle.

'This is a dirt bike,' he said throwing one leg over the top. 'It's not made for the road.' He found the kick starter and folded it out. 'So it doesn't need keys.' He slammed it down and the bike's engine vroomed into life. Rachel's eyes lit up and she cheered. Cat still didn't look convinced. 'It's okay,' he said over the noise of the engine. 'Hop on.' Cat helped Rachel up onto the seat behind him then got on herself. 'Right, now hold on tight.'

There was death and pain everywhere and Cat found it hard not to look. Some people had been killed or hurt by falling debris and their bodies or limbs lay on the road. Others had been badly burnt by the explosion and lay howling in pain. Their scorched skin stank worse than anything she had ever smelt. There were a lot of fires too. Every second or third house seemed to be either on fire or about to be. Cat watched Rachel's little head between her and Donnie and tried to squash her in tight so she couldn't see.

The high-performance dirt bike made short work of the far outer suburbs and pretty soon the houses began to thin out until finally they were clear of the city. Donnie kept on riding up into the hills, then stopped at the top of the first one where they could see right back over the many kilometres to the city. 'We'll rest here for a while, then we must ride for as long as we can.'

They stopped again just after dawn beside a creek in a little valley deep in the mountains. He turned the engine off and listened for any sign of life. Only birds and running water. Good, they could do with avoiding other people for a while. 'We'll rest here.'

Cat and Rachel sat beside the bike and Donnie got a map out of his bag. Where were they? He tried to retrace their steps. He remembered that road, yes, and that hill, then they had travelled about an hour in that direction. Great, there were mountains between them and the city. They could relax a bit. He'd read a lot about nuclear explosions over the years: they were capable of destroying whole cities in one terrific blast, but not whole countries, so there was still hope. And Sydney and Melbourne were at the bottom of the waterways so if the wind and elements favoured them the radiation might not spread that far. Donnie raised his hand to feel the wind and looked at his compass. It was blowing easterly and back toward the city. He looked around the small valley. There was a track leading up into the bush and he wondered if it might lead up onto the hills behind. Maybe he would be able to see the sky above the city from there? He would like to see it, and it would be good to stretch his legs too, after running and sitting on the motorcycle all night. The girls would be safe here for the moment.

Cat lay down with her head on her pack and watched Rachel, who curled herself up into a ball beside her. 'Why don't you come and put your head up here?' The child moved up and put her head on Cat's chest and Cat stared stroking her gently. 'Are you glad we stopped for you?' Rachel nodded. She was playing with the material on Cat's top and stopped for a moment to look up at the trees as a large bird flew over top of them and perched on a branch above them.

'Look,' she said, pointing up.

'Yes. Ah, Rachel …' Cat wanted to ask her about her parents or to maybe talk about what had happened in Sydney. Maybe Rachel didn't understand? But they looked into each other's eyes and Cat understood that questions weren't necessary. She smiled and Rachel smiled back.

Donnie walked for half an hour, then for another fifteen minutes up the hill. He had been watching the time carefully. It wouldn't do to leave Cat and Rachel for too long. Not today. There might be other people in these trees, scared, desperate and dangerous. He had to be careful. He was getting tired now too, and he had to be responsible. He walked a little further and, just as his watch ticked over an hour, came to the top. The hills in front of him rolled a long way into the distance, then dropped invisibly to the city somewhere below. Thick black smoke sat above it in a dark cloud. He could see flashes of orange and yellow reflected from below. Sydney was burning. He had read once that the blast at Hiroshima had left shadows on the walls of where people had been in their last seconds. Shadows and nothing else but pain and loss and death. How could it have come to this? He wiped the tears from his face. He couldn't do this now. It was time to keep living, to survive.

On the way back down the hill he took a wrong turn and walked for fifteen minutes in the wrong direction before realising his mistake. Angry at himself, he turned back up the hill and after another twenty minutes found the right track again. He was frustrated and walking faster and faster down the hill when he stopped dead in his tracks. There were voices in the trees. He crouched down and listened. They were not far away. He was almost at the bottom of the valley, so they must be close to the creek. Without thinking, he started forward through the bush till he saw a flash of white through the trees. There was a caravan, a big one, with an awning out the side. He could see a man moving now, cooking sausages on a barbecue. The smell was so good it was almost painful. A woman's voice yelled out from the caravan. Donnie watched the man carefully. He seemed harmless enough, middle-aged perhaps, with thinning grey hair and a stocky, if not slightly overweight, build. Maybe he should introduce himself: they might even give him something hot to take back to the girls. He watched the woman when she came out. She seemed friendly too, happy. Maybe they didn't know about the bomb? It was possible. It was a long way over the hills and it might not have woken them in the middle of the night, and if they didn't have a radio ... Donnie moved his foot and it caught a dead branch lying in the foliage. It snapped and the two people looked around. They seemed to be looking straight at him. There was suspicion in their eyes and he was glad he hadn't revealed himself.

When Donnie got back he found Rachel curled up into Cat and them both asleep beside the bike. His heart beat a little easier as he stood watching them. They looked very comfortable, and very peaceful – better to pass this ghastly day in sleep than to be awake and tormented by its horrors. He took out his pack, propped it up against the back wheel of the bike and sat down. He had never really shared Cat's burning desire to have children. He had found so much joy in his work and in their life together. And yet, watching them together now, he could understand a little more about family and how it might feel, and he liked it. There they were, just two people, one he had lived with for years and one he'd known for just a few hours, and they were all he had in the world and that was enough. He checked the wind again, then felt his eyes closing. He hadn't been asleep in more than two days, but he must stay awake ...

MICK AND BEV

Mick, a forty-six-year-old plumber from Parramatta with big plump red checks and a smile that went from ear to ear, had told this wife Bev three weeks ago that Sydney would be bombed and that the best thing they could do would be to pack up the caravan, fill some jerry cans with gas and water and head out of the city until it had all blown over. He'd been saying the same thing to anyone else who would listen to, and even invited some of their friends to join them. None of them came. But Bev knew her husband's uncanny record for being right about things like this, so they filled up their caravan with everything they thought they might need for a month or two in the bush, and drove for three days until they found a spot they liked and set up camp.

Both of them had heard the explosion in the night and lay in the dark in the caravan holding each other until Bev went back to sleep. In the hours that followed, Mick lay in the darkness, drifting in and out of nightmares about what might be happening over the hills. After breakfast the next morning he sat thinking. He had a faint idea that he had heard an engine not far off in the early hours and something had moved in the trees when he was cooking this morning. He finished the cup of coffee. Maybe he should go and have a look around? He was probably being a bit paranoid, but there seemed no harm in being cautious.

Two hundred metres down the creek he found Donnie, Cat and Rachel all asleep beside their motor bike. He watched them for a moment in silence until Donnie stirred and opened his eyes.

SHANE AND MALCOLM

In the morning Shane stirred and sat up in the berth. He looked first out the window then around the cabin. Yes, they were out at sea, and no, it wasn't a dream. There was the prime minister sitting at the tiller steering the boat. He, too, had heard the bomb in the night, but he hadn't wanted to talk about it then. It was too loud, too terrible. He put his head out of the cabin into the morning air and looked at Malcolm. 'Didn't you go to bed at all?' he asked.

'No, and I think I'm getting the hang of this sailing business now.'

'So I suppose you'll be wanting some breakfast then, sailor?'

'Have you got something?'

'Oh yeah. I've got lots of things – I've got bacon in a can, sausages, baked beans, bread, eggs, hash browns. I've even got a cold beer to wash it all down, if you're interested.' Shane held up a can of beer.

Malcolm smiled. 'No thanks, but breakfast sounds pretty good.'

Shane cooked them breakfast in the crammed kitchen. He didn't have much crockery, so he had to eat out of a pot lid after giving Malcolm his only plate. They ate in silence. Later Shane looked at the shore, then went back down below and fished out his charts. 'That's Jervois Bay,' he said. 'Wow. You've done well to sail down this far on your own.'

Malcolm grinned. 'Not bad for an old bugger, huh?'

That night it was Shane's turn to sit up late, partly because it seemed like the only way to get Malcolm away from the tiller and downstairs for some rest, but mostly because he had a lot to think about. Everything had changed. What was he going to do now? He'd spent a lot of money these last few days on food, and added to the other supplies he'd stocked up with, it should keep him for maybe a month after Canberra if he rationed it. But what then?

In the morning they looked at the charts again together: they must be off the coast of Ulladulla somewhere. They were making excellent time. Malcolm, refreshed from his sleep, made them breakfast and after they had eaten they sat chatting on the cockpit.

'How come you haven't got a girlfriend?' Malcolm asked.

'Me?'

'Yeah.'

'Girls don't like guys like me.'

'What do you mean guys like you?'

'I mean bums.'

'You're not a bum, Shane. Why do you think that?'

'Well, I don't actually. It's all right for people to think and do things differently to everybody else, that's what I think, but try telling them that. For them it's all about money and sex appeal and stuff like that and I just don't care about any of it.'

'You don't care about sex?' The prime minister found this a little hard to believe.

Shane smiled. 'Well yeah, I guess I care about that, but I'd get too screwed up if I worried about all the things in this life that I don't get.'

When Shane was downstairs doing the dishes Malcolm put his head through the door. 'Hey, you got a radio on this thing?'

'Yeah, sure. It's right there – put it on if you like.' Malcolm fiddled with the tuner until a hazy static-filled voice filled the cabin.

Melbourne and Sydney had been completely destroyed. New York, Los Angeles and over thirty other American cities had been bombed by the Chinese. Beijing, Shanghai, Hong Kong, and many more centres across Asia had been bombed by the United States. Almost every major city in Europe had been hit too, including London, Paris, Moscow and Berlin. In the smaller Australian cities there were riots, looting and fires. In Canberra things were even worse. The prime minister's house had been attacked and his family and all other ministers had fled to an undisclosed location. The prime minister himself was presumed dead, along with almost seven million other people who had been in Sydney and Melbourne. In his absence, martial law had been declared by the remaining ministers in Canberra and all members of a special force had been called together to ensure the safety of the remaining cities. 'And on this day,' the narrator continued, in a more philosophical tone, 'on this terrible morning we cannot help but question our leaders. The words they spoke and the promises they made. Could all this have been prevented? Could Mr Baxter have saved Australia?'

Shane stood up and turned the radio off. Malcolm didn't want to look up at him in case he, too, hated him, but when he finally did Shane had only sympathy in his eyes. 'I'm sorry,' he said putting a hand on the older man's shoulder.

Later in the day they drifted towards land and Shane anchored them just a couple of hundred metres off-shore. Both of them sat up late and some time in the early hours Malcolm put the radio on again. The voice was a little clearer than before. 'A shadow government has been formed in Brisbane headed by the remaining ministers, and in an attempt to ensure calm and to curtail the rioting Michelle Baxter has been addressing the nation.' Malcolm turned around. Shane was looking down through the doorway. 'Okay then,' he said. 'So let's turn this baby around and head to Brisbane.'

DONNIE, CAT, RACHEL, MICK AND BEV

At first Donnie had been reluctant to accept Mick's invitation to come and eat with him and Bev at their camp. But Mick had explained that they would be doing him a great favour as his wife needed some distraction. There was something nice about the guy up close, Donnie thought. Cat and Rachel seemed to like him too.

When Bev met them at the door Donnie could see her face change a little from sadness to curiosity and was glad they had come.

'He said it would happen,' she told them later. 'That's why we're here. If only our friends had listened. If only they'd all bloody listened.' She started to cry, but pushed Mick away before he could put his arms around her, and sat down on the doorstep of the caravan. Then Rachel walked forward and put her hand on the woman's shoulder. 'It's all right, lady,' she said. 'It will all be okay.' Bev looked at the little girl for a long time.

'This is Rachel,' said Cat.

'Hello Rachel,' said Bev, wiping her eyes a little. 'I suppose you must have had quite a day.' Rachel nodded and Bev smiled a bit more. 'I bet you must all be hungry. What do you say, Mick, we'd better get some food into these people, huh?'

'Yeah. That's the spirit, Bev,' he said, putting his hand under her elbow to help her up.

'Okay,' she said, on her feet again and wiping away the rest of the tears. And soon she had them in clean clothes, washed up with a plate of hot food in front of them.

When they had eaten, they started to talk about how they had escaped and about what they should all do now. Donnie spoke of his reluctance to be near other people for a while and Mick agreed. Donnie also talked about the possible problem with fallout. It was unlikely to affect them now that it had been more than twelve hours and the wind was still easterly, but it was best all the same that they get as far away from the city as possible. Later, they began getting ready to leave.

'Where do you think you're going?' asked Bev.

'To find somewhere to camp.'

'Where?'

'Back by the river, I guess.'

'Oh no you don't.' She looked at Mick and he nodded. 'You'd better stay with us, I think.'

Donnie and Cat looked at each other, then at Rachel who had fallen asleep in the doorway of the caravan.

'Okay, yes, thank you. She'll be very pleased,' Cat said. 'She seems to like it here and I wasn't looking forward to waking her.'

'She's really something, huh?'

'Oh yeah.'

In the morning Bev woke up early and left the caravan without waking the others. She found a seat on a rock just outside the camp and sat down. Funny, she thought, how in a world where so much had happened, where so much of the life she'd had could be no more, that her thoughts should be filled with these new people she'd only just met. Donnie's initial coldness had been explained when he spoke of his reluctance to trust people right now and the dire need for caution, but what about the girl? For some reason she didn't seem to fit the pair. Rachel and Cat obviously got on well, but it wasn't like a normal mother-daughter relationship; it didn't have that comfort. Cat seemed almost mesmerised by the girl. It was as if they didn't really know each other at all or had only just met.

Bev could hear footsteps inside the caravan. It was Rachel. She stopped in the door a moment, then came out into the awning and stared down at Donnie and Cat, who were asleep on the blow-up mattress. She stood there for a full five minutes before she turned and caught Bev watching her.

'Hello. How long have you been watching me?' she said, moving toward her.

'Not long. Did you have a good sleep?'

'Yes thank you.'

'You're a very polite little girl, aren't you?'

Rachel nodded. 'Yes.'

'Did Donnie and Cat teach you such good manners?'

'No.' Rachel came right up and stood closer to her.

'Did you learn them at school?'

'No. I don't go to school yet. Mum and Dad said I have to wait for ...'

'For what?'

'Ah ... for Daddy to finish his work.'

'So Donnie's not your daddy?'

'No.' Bev took a big breath.

'Was your daddy in the fire yesterday?'

'I don't know. He was out of town and Mummy went to look for him and she didn't come back.'

'And they left you all by yourself?'

'No. Judy the babysitter was there, but then she left and didn't come back as well.'

'You must have been very scared?'

'Yes.'

'And that's when Cat and Donnie found you?'

'Yes.'

'Oh, you poor thing. Come here.' Rachel stepped forward and Bev put her arms around her. They stayed like that for a long time. 'Now, how about we cook everybody some breakfast, just you and me?'

Rachel nodded. It was nice to have so many adults around. Mummy and Daddy had been putting her in that horrible childcare centre all day since she could remember and when they did pick her up before dinner they were always too rushed or tired to be nice.

Mick and Donnie and Cat all woke to the smell of breakfast cooking on the barbecue. The mood was a little lighter than the day before and after they'd eaten Mick brought out his radio and they searched the frequencies until they could hear a voice. It spoke of the destruction and of the provisional government and the exodus to Brisbane.

'No,' said Donnie, when Mick had turned the radio off and they all seemed to be looking at him. 'It's where everyone will be going, and we have to stay on our own for as long as we can.'

'But what about food?' said Bev. 'We can't stay here forever. And if that's where the food will be in three weeks or a month, then better we make the trip while we have enough food for five of us to get there.' Bev looked at Cat then at Rachel. 'And besides. I think someone else has got another reason to go up there.'

Cat looked at Rachel then at Bev. 'You mean her parents? You think?'

'Yes. I think from what she's told me there's a chance they might be in Brisbane.'

Rachel blushed a little when she looked at Cat. For some reason she felt she was betraying her somehow, but Cat only looked back at her a moment, then smiled too.

'No, Donnie, I agree,' she said. 'If Brisbane is where the survivors are heading then so must we. Surely if we stay well clear of Sydney we'll be all right.'

Donnie watched Cat for a moment, examining her determination, and when her face didn't change he started to nod his head.

'Okay, okay, then we'll head north to Brisbane.'

'Together,' Bev added, nudging Mick who had fallen silent.

'Yes,' he agreed limply. 'Together.' All of a sudden he had a very bad feeling about it.

SHANE AND MALCOLM

Out on the water Shane and Malcolm weren't alone: a lot of other boats had fled the bomb and some, already at sea, had escaped it by chance. The team from Rodger, Smith and West, a downtown investment bank, had chartered the entire fleet of a Darling Harbour yacht company for a five-day isolated team-building exercise when, on the fourth night, the sky west of them was lit up a little after midnight. The young executives, high on booze and sex and pills, had sobered up pretty quickly. Their food and water would be gone in a day, and none of them could sail well enough to get far; they'd been using the motors mainly and they were all almost out of diesel. In the morning they pulled all the boats together and sat around the table in the largest cabin. Some of the women had been crying all night. The men were scared, too.

James Smith Junior sat sternly at the head of the table. It was time, he decided, to take charge. No one had ever really liked

Smith much – there was something ruthless and cruel and spoilt about him – but they listened now.

'We have to get more food and water,' he said. 'And we have to do it fast. We'll send out an SOS on the radio and see who comes.'

'But what can they do? They can't share their food with us. There are too many of us.'

'They can and they will, one way or another.' They could all see the coldness in his eyes and none of them liked it, but they could think of no other way.

Malcolm and Shane were the third boat to answer the SOS. The first was an older couple. They hadn't questioned the call when they saw the six vessels all in perfect floating order and Smith had had them taken prisoner and their rations taken into the big cabin. The second pair to answer the call were a young German couple who'd been out of touch with the outside world for the last six weeks of their journey across the South Pacific from South America. They weren't so easily taken in, putting up a good fight when the dozen or so twenty-somethings jumped aboard their vessel. Daniel Thomson, who had been responding particularly well to Smith's orders, took care of the executions. The others were horrified, but they helped load the dead couple's food onto the big yacht and smashed a hole in the bottom of the hull to sink the boat and the bodies.

It was the second morning after the explosions when Shane and Malcolm saw the flotilla on the horizon.

'They don't look like they're sinking,' said Shane, squinting across the water.

'No,' agreed Malcolm. 'I'll grab the binoculars.'

'What you reckon?' asked Shane.

'I don't like it.'

'Neither do I,' said Shane, 'but we have to go – it's the law of the sea.'

Daniel Thomson, watching the boat coming towards them, had to rub his eyes twice and look again to make sure he wasn't seeing things.

'What is it?' the others asked.

'Not what, who.'

'Who is it?'

'You're not going to believe this,' he said, looking at Smith. 'It's Malcolm fucken Baxter.'

'The prime minister?' When Daniel nodded, Smith snatched up the binoculars.

'So what do we do now?' asked one of the others.

Smith looked at him sternly. 'We stick to the plan.'

Shane went up the bow with the binoculars to get a closer look at the group. There were a lot of them. They were rich-looking, desperate too. When he waved, a few of them waved back.

'Ahoy,' Smith yelled when they were close enough to hear.

'Ahoy,' Shane replied, looking at Smith standing in front of the others. He watched him carefully. He didn't like rich people, especially not rich, cocky people with big shiny teeth like in the movies.

'Welcome,' yelled Smith. 'Come aboard. We have food and supplies to share.'

'So what did you send out an SOS for?' replied Shane. Smith didn't seem to hear the question and Shane turned and glanced at Malcolm again. They were close now, just a few metres away, and one of the people on the flotilla extended out a long plastic pipe. Shane took it and they started to pull the boat in. A couple of them almost had a hold of their side when by chance something in the water caught Shane's eye.

There was a yacht below them, an older and much bigger yacht, submerged just a few metres below the surface of the water. He looked closer. Yes, there was a face in the window. A dead white face. He looked back up at Smith and saw his eyes plainly now. He'd seen Shane look down, too. Gripping the pipe tightly, Shane pushed it away with all his might and their boat just missed the grip of the hands reaching at it from the flotilla. 'Start the engine,' he yelled back at the prime minister. 'We're getting the hell out of here. Go!' Malcolm was already on his feet and pulling the rip cord for the engine. It burst into life and they began to move away.

'Wait, wait.' There were yells from the yachts and a couple of splashes as some of them dived into the water. 'Take us with you. Take us with you.'

When they'd put some miles between them and the flotilla Shane and Malcolm began to relax a little again.

'Close shave, huh?' Shane laughed.

'Bloody hell.' Malcolm laughed too.

'I think we should head into land,' Shane suggested while they ate dinner that night.

'You think it's safe after that?'

'I'm not sure. Possibly not, but the water's getting low so we're going to have to go in sooner or later.'

Malcolm agreed. 'And maybe we should keep watches now too?'

After everything that had happened, it was nice to have company. And besides, Malcolm had become quite fond of Shane.

In the morning they were close to shore, looking for a place to land. 'We don't need much,' Shane explained. 'This thing has a liftable keel and it's light as, so we can take it right up onto the beach.' After an hour they found a quiet bay where the small beach was bordered by green, tree-covered hills. Shane ran the boat right up onto the beach and dug the anchor into the sand. Then they took out the main water tank and anything else that looked as if it might hold water, and set out. They walked for an hour before they found a creek.

They loaded all the water onto the boat, but didn't cast off again until late afternoon when they heard voices and footsteps running down through the trees toward them.

DONNIE, CAT, RACHEL, MICK AND BEV

Mick emptied two of his jerry cans of petrol into the tank then drove them slowly over the hills. The gravel roads were narrow and he had to be careful of the caravan around the corners. Cat watched Rachel play with a toy Bev had found her in the back and beside her Donnie stared out the window. The wind in the trees still seemed to be blowing easterly. After an hour or so they came to a larger road and there were people.

'Look,' Rachel said. 'What's wrong with them?' Donnie wound up his window, locked his door and made the others do the same. The people on the road parted for their car and turned toward them, but didn't seem able to see them somehow.

'They must have been blinded by the flash,' Donnie said.

'How do they know where to go?' Rachel asked.

'They don't. They're probably all just following each other.'

'Oh, how terrible. Are you sure we can't help some of them?'

'No,' said Donnie sternly. 'We can't risk it.'

'I'm scared,' said Rachel.

Donnie put his arm around her. 'Why don't you close you eyes for a while, okay?'

They drove slowly through the people for about an hour and then the road seemed to get busier, with more people who had to stand aside to let them through. Some of them could see, and yelled things at them as they passed: 'Hey, stop. Help. Give us a ride.' They tried to get into the caravan, too.

Finally they turned again onto a bigger road that led to the motorway. They stopped on the bridge above to look down. The lanes were all empty. They watched for a few minutes and not a single car went past. Mick and Bev both turned around and looked at Donnie. 'I think we should risk it. It doesn't make sense that it should be empty after what the radio said, but it's better that we get as far away from here as we can and this is definitely the fastest way.'

Mick pushed the big car gently up to a hundred and they drove for a full hour. 'Every kilometre further we get is a blessing,' said Donnie, not quite believing their clear run.

Around a corner the road dipped into a small valley and on the other side there was a roadblock. The men at the top of the hill wore yellow suits that covered their entire bodies.

'Who are they?' asked Bev.

'I'm not sure,' Donnie replied. 'Some kind of containment crew?'

'What will they do?' asked Cat.

'I don't know.'

'I don't like the look of them,' said Cat. 'They don't look very friendly.'

'I don't either,' agreed Bev.

'Will they try and hurt us?' asked Rachel.

Mick sat up in the front seat. 'Just you let them try,' he said.

'Let's turn around and go the other way. Come on, Mick.' He started turning the wheel but Bev stopped him. 'No, wait. They've seen us – look, two of them are walking down the road.'

'What should we do?'

'Wait,' said Donnie. 'They'll chase us now if we run. Just try and keep calm and let's see what happens.' The men were halfway down the hill now.

'I'm getting out,' said Mick.

'No,' said Bev, trying to grab his arm. 'It's too dangerous.'

'Stiff,' said Mick. 'I want to talk to them and see what they're up to before I let them come up close to our camp. If anything happens you lot get the hell out of here.'

'Wait Mick ...' Bev objected again but Mick had already shut the door behind him.

He met the men about 50 metres in front of the car.

'Why have you stopped?' said one of them through an electronic speaker. 'You must proceed to the top of the hill for processing.'

'Processing? I'm not sure I like the sound of that. What if we don't want to be processed?'

'Sir, I'm afraid you have no choice,' said the same man, stepping forward and reaching to take Mick by the arm. Mick pulled back.

'Who says we haven't got a choice?' The men didn't answer. Mick glanced back at the car. 'What if we go back?'

'Sir, that's impossible. Sydney has been declared a quarantined area and no one's allowed to go back. You and your family must come to the top of the hill for processing. You don't have any other choice.' This time both men caught Mick's arms, but he threw his closed fist into the stomach of one, pushed the other over, then turned and started back toward the car. He was almost back, and watching their shocked faces through the windscreen, when one of the men took a gun from his belt and shot Mick in the back. He fell dead on the road just metres in front of the car. The blood drained from Bev's face, her mouth opened wide and her head shook in disbelief.

Donnie leapt over into the front, started the engine and, with his foot hard down on the accelerator, swung the car around, the caravan lurching behind it. As shots rang out in the air behind them he pushed the big old V8 for everything it could give them. In the rear-vision mirror he could see people starting to move away from the partitions off the road to chase them.

He took the first exit off the motorway, then turned again down the first road, then again down another and another. The yellow suits would have faster vehicles so their best hope was to lose them before they could see where they'd gone. He took three more turns left and right into the bush and when the road had turned to gravel and got too thin to carry on he stopped.

'I think we'll be okay now,' he said. 'I don't think they'll find us here.'

When they'd caught their breath they looked at Bev. She was pale and looking straight ahead. They got out of the car to leave her alone for a moment.

'I'm scared,' said Rachel, tugging at Cat's side. Cat picked her up and perched her on her hip. 'Don't worry. It will be all right. I think we lost them, didn't we Donnie?'

Donnie had walked up the road a little way behind them and seemed to be concentrating. He turned around and looked at her. 'They're coming.'

She listened: there was a gentle roar of multiple engines getting louder.

Bev had got out of the car and held the keys out in front of her. 'Get the motor bike out,' she said.

'There's no time. And it can only take three,' Donnie protested.

'Get it out,' she said again. 'There's time.' Bev had a strange look of determination about her that made Donnie listen. 'The road ends for me here.'

'No, Bev, you must go on.' But there was no time to argue. The engines were getting louder. Donnie kicked the bike over and the other two got on. Bev stood in the middle of the road behind the car and caravan to block their pursuers' way. Donnie went forward a bit then turned the bike so they could see her. She seemed to be staring at Rachel. A faint smile had come over her face.

Donnie held the throttle right around and they sped down the hill away from Bev and the caravan, but the bike soon started to miss. The engine cut out, came back to life, then cut out and refused to start again.

'What's wrong? What's the matter with it?' Cat asked as they slowed down to a stop.

'I don't know. I think it's out of gas.' He took off the petrol cap and looked inside.

'Shit.'

'What is it?'

'It's bone dry.' Donnie looked behind them and listened. The vehicle noises had stopped for the moment.

'They must be at the caravan.'

'Maybe they won't come any further?' But right then there was a loud crunching sound and Rachel started crying again. Donnie looked around quickly.

'We'll stash the bike in the trees, then make a run for it. Quick, down here.'

They followed a thin track into the bush and down a steep bank.

'Maybe they'll pass?' suggested Cat. They could hear the heavy vehicles slow down. 'Please pass.'

But the engines had stopped.

'They must have found the bike,' said Donnie.

And now they could hear heavy footsteps.

'They're coming. Let's go.'

The track carried on down then suddenly came out onto a beach. They ran quickly out onto the sand.

DONNIE, CAT, RACHEL, SHANE AND MALCOLM

'We should help them,' said Shane.

'No, wait. We don't know what they're running from.'

'There,' Shane said, pointing. The men in the yellow suits were rushing down the hill in single file.

Malcolm looked at Donnie and Cat and yelled as loud as he could, 'Swim, swim.' Then, 'Start the engine. We have to pick them up,' he said to Shane.

Donnie and Cat didn't hesitate: they started swimming toward the boat. Shane gave Malcolm the tiller, grabbed the longest thing he could find and went up onto the bow. 'We need to get as close to them as we can,' he yelled back at Malcolm.

The men were almost down at the beach now. They didn't have much time. Shane stuck the pole out as far as he could. They missed it the first time and the boat almost passed them but then Donnie grabbed it and Shane pulled them in close and helped them up out of the water.

'Go! Go!' he yelled to Malcolm. The men were on the beach now. Some of them had guns. 'Inside! ' he yelled. 'Get inside the cabin, quick.' Shane pushed them in and told Malcolm to get in there too, then wedged the throttle on full and took a rope lead from the tiller to steer the boat and jumped into the cabin himself just as the guns started firing. Water splashed up around the boat. A wire split above them and a window smashed, but they were soon out of range.

'That was close,' said Malcolm to Donnie.

'Too close. I thought we were for it then. Who were those people? They stopped us at a road block on the motorway and killed our friend.'

'There were four of you?'

'Five. We had to leave Bev at the top of the hill and make a run for it on the bike. Then we ran out of gas, and they kept chasing us.'

'They were the Twelve O'clockers,' said Malcolm. 'I'd wondered when we might cross their path.'

'I've just realised who you are,' Donnie interrupted. 'This is amazing.'

Malcolm frowned, then continued.

'The Twelve O'clockers are a radical right-wing group that have been preparing, accumulating weapons and supplies for this day for a long time. My government tried to disband them several times but they only disappeared underground – until last week, when they resurfaced in greater numbers than we'd ever estimated. We've been getting reports that they were gathering at the city borders. They wear yellow to signal the light of a new day when they believe fire will come to earth and burn all the sinners away.'

'And so their new day has come?' asked Cat. Malcolm did not answer. 'And they won't be the only maniacs out there looking to inflict their will.' Shane remembered Smith's eyes on the boat and the face in the water. 'It's a very dangerous and uncertain time.'

'So what about the National Guard then? Where are they and what are they going to do about these Twelve O'clockers?' asked Donnie.

'The NG will have many problems to deal with right now,' Malcolm replied.

'So at the moment the way north is blocked?' said Donnie.

'The way by land,' Shane smiled. 'I'll get you some towels and some dry clothes'

A while later, Donnie, Cat and Rachel were dressed in Shane's T-shirts and ripped jeans. Rachel's went down to her ankles and she wore a big pair of woollen rugby socks underneath. She was still visibly upset by their ordeal and hadn't spoken yet. Donnie and Shane left her and Cat alone and went back up on deck.

'So they will kill us all if they find us?' Donnie asked Malcolm.

'If they find us. Yes, they'll kill us all. As far as I know they'll kill anyone who comes out of the city, or even anyone they think has come into contact with people that were in the city at the time of the explosion.'

Donnie thought about this a moment, then leaned toward Malcolm. 'That's why the National Guard aren't taking over, isn't it? They're going to let this group stop the spread of radiation, aren't they?'

Malcolm was silent.

'Did they see you?' Donnie asked, sitting back.

'No,' said Shane. 'I watched to make sure.'

'Then that's something at least.'

'Have they got boats?' Shane asked.

'By the sound of it they can use anything they want to use.'

'Then we just have to hope they have bigger fish to fry,' Shane suggested.

Malcolm was looking out to sea. 'What's the range on this thing?' he asked.

'Anywhere if she's got enough supplies and crew with the nerve.'

'Well, we just filled it with water, didn't we?'

'Yes, but that's only 50 litres plus the other 10 or so we put in other bottles. That would only last five people about a week. And the food probably wouldn't hold out even for that long.'

'What about New Zealand?'

Shane shook his head. 'No way. It's too far. It would take at least three weeks of good sailing in a boat this size.'

'Are there any other islands closer?'

'Yes, but not any with food on them, and even if there were, who's to say they'd let us come ashore after all this?'

'So what then?' Donnie asked.

Malcolm thought for a moment. 'We carry on. Brisbane's where we have to go and Shane's right, we just have to hope that we don't cross their path again.'

'A lot of people will be trying to go north,' said Shane. 'And they'll be pretty busy keeping everyone back.'

'What if they don't let us into Brisbane?' said Cat who'd come up from the cabin.

'Then we deal with that then,' replied Malcolm.

'How is the girl?' Donnie asked.

Cat frowned. 'Rachel's not well. She's cold and clammy. I think she might have a fever.'

'Why don't we let her rest for a while then,' Malcolm suggested. 'She's probably in shock and it was cold in the water. Put her under the covers and I'll make her a hot cup of Milo.'

In the morning they started sailing north. It was easier with four of them taking turns. They could have all the sails out and with a tail wind most of the way they started to make pretty good time.

On the third night Malcolm woke suddenly.

'What is it?' asked Shane, who was awake and looking at him across the cockpit.

'I don't know. I just had a sudden pain in my side.'

'Are you all right?'

'Yes. I think so.' Malcolm was lying. The pain had been bad, but worse still, he felt different now, as though he were somehow diminished. He lay awake, looking up at the sky and wondering about his family.

Donnie and Cat had been waking a lot, too. Rachel was getting worse: her face was flushed most of the time and she hardly ate or got out of bed. 'She needs a doctor,' Cat had started saying. 'We need to get to Brisbane soon or she's not going to make it.' And so they sailed faster and for longer, sometimes almost all night. The food was running low now, too. They only had enough for a couple more days.

'We will be there in the morning.' Shane said on the fourth night after dinner when everyone had been waiting eagerly as he looked over the charts. 'Probably about ten o'clock.'

'And not a minute too soon.' Cat said, looking at Rachel who had not got out of bed all that day.

They didn't find the mouth of the Brisbane river until late afternoon. 'We made it,' said Shane, pulling the engine cord. 'We'll drop the sails and motor up.' He sat at the tiller and Malcolm went up to the bow of the boat. There was something strange about the water. It was darker than usual and smelt funny. They kept hitting things too, but they were submerged and he couldn't see what they were. He returned to the cockpit.

'There's something wrong.' The air was foul, as if the river were full of manure and it was getting worse by the minute until they felt almost like vomiting.

'Where are all the people?' Cat asked, holding her noise. The river got narrower as they came up to the corner before the CBD. None of them had been looking at the houses on either side of the river, which had been getting slowly darker and darker. All of a sudden, they came around the bend – the once busy city of Brisbane was no more. Its buildings lay in dark clumps and the ones that still stood seemed to hang in the air like great black skeletons. Horrified, Malcolm looked over the side again. He could see what was in the water now. There was a face, black and burnt. An old lady with floating grey hair. He looked at the others and quickly covered his nose too. 'It's burnt flesh.'

'When did it happen?' asked Shane.

'Three nights ago,' Malcolm answered, remembering the pain that woke him in the night.

'The Chinese must have known everyone would come here and waited for them all to arrive.'

'It's called dirty bombing,' added Donnie.

'But surely they had all killed each other before that?'

'They probably had. They have launch tubes deep inside mountains and in submarines and on ships, all set to launch even if there is no one there to fire them. People don't like to lose.'

'It's all so silent,' Cat said. 'I don't like it.'

'No, let's get the hell out of here.' Shane swung the boat around and let the fast-moving current carry them back out.

Even when they were well past the heads, he let the boat go on drifting out to sea for a while. He half wanted to ask Malcolm which way to turn, but he had been sitting quietly up on the bow since they'd come out of the river and Shane didn't want to interrupt him. Donnie and Cat were sitting in the cabin beside Rachel.

'She's getting worse,' Donnie said. 'We have to find a doctor before it's too late.'

'How long do you think we have?'

'I'm not sure. Two days, maybe three.'

'We'll go north then,' said Shane standing up. 'We'll set sail and go north.'

'But what about food and water?'

'We'll go ashore. We'll raid an orchard or a farm or something. The Sunshine Coast isn't far away.'

For most of the afternoon Donnie and Shane took turns at sitting at the tiller and trimming the sails. Would Malcolm come back to them? Could he, after all that had happened? Things would be a lot harder without him. But he had lost everything he lived for and it would be a lot easier just to give up. By late afternoon, though, Malcolm got up and said he'd make them a cup of coffee, then take a turn at the tiller.

'It's radiation poisoning, isn't it?' Cat said when Donnie went down and sat beside her.

He nodded.

'She must have had a lower tolerance than us, poor thing.'

'How long till we can get her help?'

'I don't know, tomorrow maybe.'

'Will she make it?'

He picked up her hand, but didn't answer.

None of them passed that night easily. Malcolm had only just decided to stay with the others. All afternoon he had wanted it all to end; to drop off the side of the boat, sink to the bottom and be free of his mind and conscience.

There were too many questions. What if he hadn't supported the

Americans? Would they have been bombed anyway? What if he'd left the decision up to someone else? And what if he hadn't have left his family? Would they have gone to Brisbane anyway? Did they know about dirty bombing? Did they know it was coming? Did they suffer? He remembered how much it had hurt when he woke in the night. Was that their pain? Had it hurt them that much? The sea shimmered peacefully in the moonlight. If it wasn't for the little girl in the cabin he would be down there now, away from every thought.

Donnie kept waking to check on Rachel and Cat, who sat beside her on the floor. He rested a little easier for a while when he saw Cat's head had dropped onto the bed and that she was asleep.

Shane didn't sleep at all. He sat up in the cockpit, propped by his pillow, staring up at the stars. He'd been thinking about his parents a lot since he got the boat. Little things would remind him of them. The clearest memory was of when he must have been only about five. He was standing up the front of the boat looking out at the horizon. It was late in the day and the last golden rays of the sun were shining through the clouds. His dad had come up behind him. 'Enjoy it, son,' he'd said. 'People will tell you a lot of things in your life, and some of them you'll want to believe. But if you always remember to enjoy this, then you'll never have nothing. This is the real gold.'

Things had just got harder and harder after they died. Everyone seemed so angry with him or in too much of a hurry. No one had time. Well, his friends did sometimes, but they grew up so fast and became adults too, and he didn't want to be one yet. He didn't want to have no time. Still, he thought, looking down into the cabin, it wasn't that nice being on the outside either. He remembered how safe and warm he'd felt with his parents. Would he ever feel that again?

In the morning they ate the last of Shane's food.

'We have to go back onto land today,' he said.

'How far north do you think we are? Are we near Colum Beach?'

'No. I looked at the charts. It would take another full day's sailing, maybe two.'

'And we don't have the diesel to motor up there?'

'No. We used almost all that we had left getting up the river.'

Donnie sighed, looking over at Cat and Rachel. 'So be it.'

Mid-afternoon they found a small sandy beach ringed by a low cliff.

'Who will go?' Cat asked when they'd raised the keel and run the boat up onto the sand.

'Shane and I will go,' Donnie said. 'We'll be the fastest.'

Malcolm stepped forward. 'Then I'll keep watch here until you get back.'

'Good,' said Donnie.

'How long will you be?'

'We'll go as fast as we can.'

Cat went back into the cabin and poured the last drops of water into a small bottle and handed it to them. Donnie kissed her. When they got to the top of the cliff they turned around and looked back at the small boat. Shane put his hand on Donnie's shoulder. 'They'll be okay. Malcolm will look after them.'

They ran for a full hour. The land was bare until they came to a small creek with a bit of green around it. 'We'll follow it upstream. Where there's water, there's life,' Donnie said.

They ran for another quarter of an hour till they come to a sheep farm. They hid behind a fence watching and catching their breath. In one of the sheds there was an old ute.

'You think the keys will be in it?'

'We'll see,' said Shane. 'Let's go.'

The doors were unlocked and Shane looked around the driver's seat for the keys.

After Midnight

'No, wait. Look,' Donnie said. 'Try that button. A lot of farmers lose their keys so they wire things up to work without them.'

Shane pushed the button and the engine started to wind over. 'Pump the gas.' He did and it started. As they passed the farmhouse Shane looked for the owners – surely if they were there they would have heard the engine. There was no one.

They followed the gravel road for a while. 'Try and remember the corners,' Donnie suggested. 'We haven't got time to get lost.' They made a couple more turns then came to a crop farm and an orchard. The farmhouse was quiet again as they went past and turned into the orchard.

They stopped beside a big shed and inside found bins full of freshly picked oranges, apples, pears, mangoes and avocados. They quickly loaded them into crates and stacked them on the back of the ute.

'Stop right there and put your hands up in the air,' said a very serious voice. 'Now turn around slowly.' A middle-aged man with grey hair and a very unfriendly, almost sarcastic, smile on his face stood a few metres away with a double-barrelled shotgun.

'So you thought you'd help yourself to old Jimmy's crop, did ya? You're not the first these last few days neither.' He seemed to be chewing on something; he brought it to the front of his mouth then spat it out. 'And I see you helped yourself to young Mr Wallace's ute and all. Well you're a couple of cheeky bastards then, aren't you? No respect for the dead. Now give me the keys and get away with you before I send you both off to apologise to him in person.'

'But, sir,' Donnie said, stepping forward, 'you don't understand.'

'What? What don't I understand? You haven't got no food so you come and steal mine so I'll starve and not you? I think I understand perfectly well, city slicker.'

'But we have a sick little girl.'

The man looked behind them in the ute. 'Where?'

'On a boat. We came up from Sydney. Me, my wife, Shane here, the little girl and Malcolm Baxter.'

'Malcolm Baxter? You mean the prime minister?'

'Yes.' Donnie hadn't meant to say Malcolm's full name, but now he wondered if it might help.

'Malcolm Baxter. He's the one that's been causing all this trouble. Bet you those men that come round in those yellow suits yesterday would like to know old Malcolm Baxter's around. Here, I don't think I'll let you two go right away after all.' He turned his head.

'Joy.' There was no reply. 'Hey Joy. You there?' He yelled louder and turned around further.

Shane seized the opportunity and leapt forward, hitting the man square on the side of the head with his closed fist. He fell to the ground.

'Max ... Max ...?' The woman's voice seemed to know something was wrong.

'Let's get the hell out of here,' Donnie said, picking up the shotgun. 'He'll be all right,' he said seeing Shane staring at the old man. 'It was a good hit, Shane, but he'll wake up again soon.'

They followed the road back to the first farm and stopped beside the farmhouse again. 'Let's find something to put water in.' said Shane. 'There'll be a tap beside the house and we can use the ute to take it back to the boat.' They looked around in the sheds and found two large black drums. The first one was empty and perfect for water. Shane took the lid off the second one and smelt inside. 'It's diesel!' They put the drum on the ute and while they filled the water beside the house Shane found more food in the back garden. He quickly dug up potatoes and carrots and picked some beans, put them in a big sack and hauled them onto the back of the ute.

He stopped again just down the road. 'What about them?' he said, looking in the paddock.

'The sheep?'

'Yeah, you think they would keep?'

'For a while.' Donnie rummaged through the glovebox and found a craft knife. The sheep bucked and kicked as they slit its throat and dragged its bleeding carcass back to the ute.

'I reckon we've done all right, you know. This lot should keep us going for ages.'

Donnie nodded, pleased with what they'd got, but he was more worried about Rachel and Cat.

There was a fence they couldn't drive through so they parked the ute and, carrying as much as they could, walked the last couple of hundred metres. When they got to the top of the cliff they knew right away that something wasn't right. It was too quiet. Donnie hurried down in front and Shane had to catch him twice when he lost his footing. They ran across the sand and onto the boat. They were gone! Shane stood in the cockpit while Donnie stared in disbelief at the empty bed.

'What the hell has happened? Where are they? They can't have just vanished. I don't believe this. It can't be happening. They must be here.' He stood up on the cockpit and yelled Cat's name. There was no answer.

Shane turned around suddenly. Something had made a splash in the water behind him. They looked over the side. Someone was swimming up to the back of the boat. A hand reached up for the stepladder.

'Malcolm! What's happened? Where are Cat and Rachel?' Donnie demanded before Shane had even helped him up.

'They took them,' he said, trying to catch his breath.

'Who?'

'The Twelve O'clockers, in yellow suits. I saw them coming down the bank and Cat told me to hide in the water and listen. I told her it wasn't safe, but she insisted. She said she wanted to plead with them. She said if she didn't get Rachel to the hospital she would die. She got worse after you left. She needed food and water. It was her only hope.'

Donnie's face had gone bright red. Shane held up a restraining hand. 'Wait.' He looked back at the prime minister. 'Malcolm, did you hear? Did they take them to the hospital?'

Malcolm was still struggling for breath. 'Yes. There were a lot of them and it took her a while to convince them but they finally agreed. She told them that she would die before they took her without promising to take the girl to a doctor. I heard them say something about Colum Beach.'

Shane had a hard time convincing Donnie that they had to load the supplies before they left. He had practically started trying to pull the sails up before Malcolm had finished talking.

'We have to wait,' he told him. 'We can't rescue them just to starve them at sea.'

'The hospital is near the beach,' Malcolm said. 'I remember visiting it on the campaign trail. I think we'll be able to get in too. They'll be guarding the food and all their supplies, but they won't be expecting anyone to break into the hospital.'

'Maybe not.'

They told Malcolm what had happened at the orchard.

'So why didn't they wait at the boat?' Donnie asked. Shane thought about this for a while. 'I don't know, maybe they didn't believe him, and they just came to check it out anyway.'

Donnie stood up. 'It doesn't matter even if they do know, I don't care, I'm going anyway.'

'So am I,' said Malcolm.

'No,' said Shane. 'You'll stay with the boat. Donnie and I will be faster without you.'

'I think you should both stay in the boat,' said Donnie. 'I'll go alone.' Shane didn't argue.

Dusk turned to dark and sometime after midnight they turned

into shore. Malcolm held the tiller while Shane and Donnie went below.

'We will wear these black beanies,' said Shane.

'I thought you weren't coming?'

'No, I am. I just didn't want to argue about it. We'll have plenty of time to do that when we all get back,' Shane said, handing Donnie the black hat before he could talk. 'And we might need a few extra bits and pieces too,' he said, hoisting a long black bag over his shoulder. 'Right,' Shane continued when they were back up on deck. 'Now Malcolm, I want you to run us right up onto the beach, then we'll push you straight back out. Head over the waves in the dark where they won't be able to see you. You can use the outboard. If you keep it below 1200 revs it shouldn't be any louder than the water. You'll see us when we come back to the beach. I'll wave this white T-shirt if we need you in a hurry, and if I want you to come back in at full revs. If we miss each other then come back at two-hour intervals until first light, then head out to sea and come back tomorrow night. Donnie, if we get separated the same rules apply.'

The little beach town was quiet and eerie. Dim lights hid behind thick curtains. Strangers weren't welcome here. They stopped beside the road and Shane glanced back to watch the dark outline of the boat disappearing over the waves.

They moved from shadow to shadow. A dog barked and they tried to stay still until it stopped. Curtains opened and a face came to the window. It scanned the darkness for a minute or so then disappeared back inside. They started off again. Shane glanced back over his shoulder. The curtains had opened again. He made eye contact with a pale face. He nudged Donnie and they started to move faster. They took a left, then a right, and found a sign for the hospital.

They were almost at the gate when all of a sudden two or three engines seemed to start at once. They ducked behind a hedge. Three big RVs came rushing out the driveway. 'You think they're looking for us?'

'Maybe, but come on, this has got to be our best chance.'

They slipped in the gate and up to the building. The hallway inside went to the left and right and straight ahead. Shane took the left hallway and started looking in the doors. All the rooms were empty and dark. Where were all the patients? A nuclear bomb had gone off not 100 kilometres down the road, for Christ's sake! He turned and started back down after Donnie. There was no one in the first two rooms that way, either, but then in the third there were lights on and an old man and a boy lay in opposite beds on the other side of the room. Shane stopped himself in the door. A nurse, who was sitting down in a seat between them, turned and caught sight of him just as he left.

In the next room he found Donnie. He was kneeling next to Cat who was sitting on the bed looking down at Rachel and holding her hand. Shane walked a little closer, then stopped. Rachel was whiter than before and her eyes seemed empty somehow. He heard the door swing open behind him and turned to the nurse.

'Is there anything you can do?'

She shook her head. 'I'm sorry.'

Cat seemed mesmerised and did not see her.

Shane stepped back toward the door and opened it slightly. There was a faint hum in the distance.

'We have to go.' Donnie turned. 'I think they're coming back.'

Cat turned to him. 'No.'

'But Cat, if we stay ...'

'No. I don't care. I won't leave her.'

'We have to leave, Donnie,' said Shane, speaking more loudly and stepping forward. He could hear the engines behind him more plainly now. 'Come on. We can't stay here.'

'Yes. Come on, Cat. We have to go now,' he said, taking her arm.

'No,' she said. 'They said they'd let me stay with her until the end.'

'And then what?' The cars were coming back up the driveway. 'Come on. It's suicide to stay. I won't let you.'

The nurse suddenly sprang forward from Shane's side and grabbed his arm. He turned and looked into her eyes, which were bright with conviction.

'Take me with you,' she said.

Shane looked at her for a brief second. 'All right. And you two, come now. Come on.'

'No, Shane,' answered Cat calmly.

'Donnie, please, won't you at least come and save yourself?'

Donnie looked between them and seemed to take a big breath. 'No, I'll stay.'

'But you ...' Shane began but stopped suddenly. There were car doors opening and closing outside and voices in the halls. He turned to the nurse.

'There's a back way,' she said. 'Come on. I'll show you.'

Shane stopped at the door again and looked around, but there was nothing he could do. He and the nurse rushed through an adjacent room where she pulled a curtain aside and let them out onto a fire escape. They ran across a grass lawn and hid behind a low hedge, watching. A man in a yellow suit come out the back door and had a look around. He seemed to pause when he looked in their direction, and Shane wondered if he could hear their breathing or maybe see their shadows, but he turned and went back inside.

'What will they do to them?' he asked, turning to the nurse.

'I don't know. They've been taking away everyone who comes in and they don't come back.'

'You think they ...?'

'Yes. I heard them talking. They've sworn some oath or something to hold back the spread of contamination and they think that everyone who comes up from the city will spread the poison.'

'They're the Twelve O'clockers.'

'The what?'

'Malcolm told us about them.'

'Who's Malcolm?'

'Malcolm Baxter.'

'Malcolm Baxter the prime minister? When did you meet him?'

'Shush. I'll tell you about it later.' Shane pointed back at the building. The nurse looked too.

'Maybe we can ...' she stopped. They could hear voices again.

'Come on.' Shane took her by the hand and they went around the hedge to where they could see the front of the small hospital. The men in the yellow coats were pushing Donnie and Cat into the back of one of the RVs. 'Where's the girl?' He looked at the young nurse's face for a moment. 'She's dead?'

'Yes. She was too far gone. The excitement would have been too much.' A car door shut.

'We have to follow them,' he said, looking back at the vehicles. 'Have you got a car?'

'Yes, but they took everything when they came. My wallet, my bag, all my keys. They wouldn't even let me keep the keys to the drugs room.'

He looked at her a moment again. 'So you were going to be taking a ride too. Is your car still here?'

'Yes, it's over there, but ...' He had already taken her by the hand again and started toward it. In the garden he found a rock and smashed it through one of the back windows. They were in.

'Sorry,' he said, suddenly unsure of what to do next. That part had been easy, but ...

The nurse pushed him gently aside, crouched down under the dashboard and started pulling out wires. She ripped open a red and a yellow one and touched them together. Nothing. She tried a red one and a yellow one, still nothing. A red and a black ... Yes. The car turned over, and she twisted the wires together.

'Where did you learn how to do that?' he asked, taking the bag off his shoulder and getting into the driver's seat.

'I haven't always been a nurse,' she said with a wink.

They followed the RVs without their lights on and far enough back not to be seen. The pursuit took them out of the small town, along the coast, around a few bends then inland until they came around a blind corner and suddenly there was a makeshift gate blocking the road. Donnie and Cat were in the back seat of one of the RVs and two of the men in yellow were about to close the gate behind them. The others must have gone on ahead. They looked around. Shane wished he hadn't come around the corner so fast and blown their cover but it was too late to pull back now and there was no time to think 'Quick. Pass me the bag.' Shane opened the zip, flicked the headlights on to full, slammed on the handbrake and opened the door. He cocked the double-barrelled shotgun and aimed it squarely at the two yellow suits struggling to see them in the bright light. 'Hands in the air,' he said with a cough. The air was putrid, it smelt terrible, but a little familiar now, too. Black smoke was rising up into the air from somewhere behind the gate. One of the guards hesitated. 'Now, or else I'll blow you away, you butchers. Donnie, Cat, get in the car.' Cat seemed bewildered and Donnie had to all but pull her out of the RV to get her moving. Shane waited until they were in the back seat. 'Now I want you to put down your guns and get behind that gate and throw me the keys and if either of you makes a sudden move I swear it will be your last.'

'You won't get far,' one of the men said through his speaker.

'Where will you go?' started the other.

'You don't have to worry about that. Now shut up and slide the keys across the ground.' He handed the nurse the shotgun and smiled and said loud enough for them to hear. 'Now I want you to keep it aimed straight at them while we back away and if they move start shooting. Even if they just flinch.'

Shane floored the little car back towards town. The fast RVs were soon coming up behind them.

'Look!' cried the nurse. 'They're setting up a roadblock at the other end of the beach.'

'They think we're going to try and drive out of town,' said Donnie.

'How else would we get out?' asked the nurse.

Shane smiled. 'Hold on.' He went right up close to the roadblock, then pulled on the handbrake and swung the car around. He grabbed the white T-shirt from his bag and, holding it high out the window, accelerated toward the flashing lights coming from the other way.

'You're going to play chicken?' Shane held the pedal right to the floor and sped toward the other cars and when they were almost about to hit he let go of the T-shirt and gripped the wheel with both hands. The leading RV slowed down, tried to swerve too quickly at the last moment, rolled over twice and landed in the middle of the road. The other cars sped towards it.

'What did you do that for? Are you crazy?'

'We needed some time. Now keep holding on.' Shane swerved up onto the gutter, drove through the playground and took the car crashing down onto the sand. He rushed around and pulled the nurse from the car. Donnie grabbed Cat too and they rushed toward the water. The Twelve O'clockers were back in their RVs now and they could hear the engines revving.

'Where is he?' yelled Shane looking out over the waves. 'He must have gone out too far. He's going to be too late.'

'Ahoy, ahoy,' came a voice in the distance. 'Over here, over here.'

'There he is,' said Donnie, pointing down the beach.

'Run,' cried Shane. 'Run!' They all ran toward Malcolm, who was running the little yacht up onto the sand further down the beach. The RVs were on the sand now and they could hear the engines roar as the big tyres gripped the sand.

'Hurry!' yelled Malcolm, helping Cat and the nurse up onto the boat. Gunfire was coming from the RVs now. Donnie and Shane pushed all their weight into the boat and with the help of a small wave set her afloat again and turning. Bullets were landing in the water around them and another window smashed. Shane gripped the stepladder and Malcolm thrust one hand down to Donnie. With the other he pulled the throttle wide open and they went bumping back out over the waves and into the night.

SHANE AND STACY

Donnie took Cat down below, made her a cup of hot water with an orange squeezed in it, wrapped her in a blanket and sat beside her on the bed. Malcolm steered the boat and after he had found some dry clothes Shane joined him and their new guest in the cockpit.

'Hi, I'm Shane, and this is Malcolm.'

'Hey. I'm Stacy.' She turned to look curiously at Malcolm for a moment, but then smiled and turned back to Shane.

'How long had you been there?'

'In the hospital? I'd been working there for the last six months. Colum Beach is a bit out of the way, I know, but I tried working in Sydney and then Brisbane and the hospitals were just too mad so I kept on heading north till I found somewhere I liked.'

'You from Melbourne?'

'Yeah. How did you know that?'

'Just a feeling. So what happened …?'

'After the bomb? Well, when Sydney was hit not much. I heard about it on the radio and everything, and everyone in town was pretty scared. But then those men arrived in the police cars. They didn't say who they were. They didn't seem like cops, but they took over everything and told everyone to stay indoors after dark and as much as possible. They said that there were a lot of dangerous people about and that it was important for their safety that they do as they were told. Then after Brisbane got bombed the people started arriving to the hospital, some were in cars and some were on foot, but they kept taking them away.'

'The men in yellow?'

'Yes.'

'And they wouldn't let you treat them?'

'No. They took away the other two nurses and doctor too. They wouldn't even let people in the doors after a while. They hid behind them in the dark and took them away as soon as they came through the entrance.'

'Bastards.'

'A lot of them looked really sick, but heaps of them only had light radiation poisoning and would have been all right. A couple of smart ones came to the back door after it started and I managed to tell them to run.'

'They were using you?'

'Yes. And we saw where they were taking the people to, Malcolm.' There was an awkward moment of silence. Malcolm seemed to know without being told.

'Well, anyway, they kept coming until the day before yesterday then they just stopped, except for Cat and Rachel who the men let us treat. Cat told me when they left that she had made them promise and begged me to help, but the little girl was already too sick and there was nothing I could do.' They all looked down in silence for a moment.

'They must have all regrouped and made their roadblock out of Brisbane to protect the north,' Shane suggested. 'That's why they stopped coming.'

'Yes, but then you came,' Stacy said, smiling up at Shane. 'And you saved my life.'

Shane felt himself getting red. He'd noticed straight away how attractive Stacy was, and she was just about his age, too, but he'd never have guessed she would look at him as she was doing now. Malcolm looked away across the water into the night trying not to intrude on the moment, and when he looked back he winked at Shane.

When Donnie come up the stairs to the cockpit a while later they were talking easily.

'Is she asleep now?' asked Stacy. He nodded. 'She had a big knock, eh. You too. It's hard, I know. Even when you only know them for a little while. But we'll do something in the morning to mark her passing. That will help, I think.'

'Thank you,' said Donnie.

'No, thank you. If it wasn't for her bringing Rachel in then you two mightn't have come and then God knows where I'd be now.' Donnie watched Stacy turn back and stare at Shane, and he smiled at Malcolm. It was the first time that either of them had smiled in days and it made them both feel a little better.

The next morning they made a little garland out of mango and avocado and orange skins and set it afloat in memory of Rachel and they all watched it until it had disappeared over the waves. Cat had gone back into the cabin afterwards, but later in the day she came up into the cockpit and even started to join in some of the conversation.

They kept sailing slowly north. The mood was lighter now. They all had enough food and water and there probably wouldn't be any more roadblocks or men in yellow suits now, cither. Shane and Stacy sat up late, talking and getting to know each other and on the third night under the full moon, when they had stayed up till almost dawn, Shane leant across the cockpit and kissed her. They slept until midday while the others ate and sailed the boat and shared cheeky glances at the two curled up together on a blanket.

On the fifth day when the water was starting to get low Cat and Malcolm made a round of coffees and they all sat in the cockpit.

'How far north do you think we've come?' Donnie asked.

Shane looked at the charts. 'I'd say we're clear of Brisbane and the Sunshine Coast by 1000 kilometres now. We're not far south of the Great Barrier Reef. There's more fish in the water if you've noticed. Big bright ones.'

'We can eat them now, too,' added Donnie, who'd stopped them fishing so far.

'So is it safe to go inland too?' Cat asked. They all looked first at Donnie, then at Malcolm.

'Yes. They won't be looking for people this far north. We should be safe from them now.'

DONNIE AND CAT

Later that evening they ran the little yacht up onto the sand of a pretty, white, safe-looking beach and Donnie and Shane looked around for an hour just to make sure they were alone.

'It's safe. There's a little river with fresh water just over the other side of the hill, too.'

They spent the first night all camped beside the boat on the beach and all of the next day bathing and resting and cleaning. It was nice to be on land, and to have some peace for a change. Shane and Stacy were happy. So was Donnie in a way, too, but not Cat or Malcolm. Malcolm seemed troubled and spent a lot of time off down the beach by himself thinking and looking out over the waves. Cat was tired at first but after a couple of days she started taking Donnie for long walks over the hills. One afternoon they were walking up a gentle slope of green, lightly wooded land when she stopped suddenly and looked at him.

'Here,' she said. 'Let's stay right here. We could build a house and keep a garden. There's water in the creek just down there and fish in the sea.'

AFTER MIDNIGHT

'What about the others?'

'What about them? They have their own paths and they'll follow them. I'm tired, Donnie. I don't want ours to go on any further. Here we could rest and start over. Maybe even start a family?'

'We're going to stay here,' Donnie told the others when they got back to the boat.

'Why?' asked Shane surprised.

'It feels safe here, and we're tired. There's a creek so we can have water and grow food, and we found a nice place where we can make a house. We don't want to go out on the boat again. A lot has happened these last few weeks and our road has to end somewhere. It may as well be here.'

After a while it was agreed. They spared Donnie and Cat everything they could from the boat and even helped them build a little hut up the hill. Then Shane and Malcolm filled the water bottles again and they got ready to leave.

'We'll come back and help you build a proper house one day,' Shane told them. 'When we've found the end of our own paths.' He had a fairly strong feeling though, as they raised the sails and started moving away from the beach, that he would never see them again.

MALCOLM

Malcolm got quieter and quieter after they left Cat and Donnie. Shane wondered if whatever demons had been haunting him had returned. He wanted to ask, but Stacy stopped him. 'Let him be,' she insisted. But as they went further north Malcolm got even quieter and began staying at the tiller till late at night, then sleeping almost all day.

On the fifth night out from the beach something woke him. It was a clear night but he could see the moon through the porthole. He looked at Stacy beside him. Her naked skin shone silver in the moonlight. Malcolm hadn't come to bed yet. He wanted to get up and check on him, but as he moved Stacy stirred, pulled him back, and he fell asleep again. In the morning Malcolm was gone.

Shane tried to imagine his friend's last moments before he stepped off the back of the boat into the darkness. He hoped he had found some peace. Maybe he had seen his wife and daughter below the surface of the water. Maybe he believed he could still get to them. They made another garland and set it afloat. Shane watched it disappear into the distance, then turned to Stacy. 'We will be okay,' she said. He smiled, kissed her and held her close until they set sail again.